S H A D O W   W I T H O U T   A   N A M E

SHADOW

WITHOUT

A NAME

TRANSLATED BY
PETER BUSH AND ANNE McLEAN

IGNACIO

PADILLA

FARRAR, STRAUS AND GIROUX
NEW YORK

Farrar, Straus and Giroux
19 Union Square West, New York 10003

Printed in the United States of America
Originally published in 2000 by Editorial Espasa-Calpe, Spain, as *Amphitryon*
English translation originally published in 2002 by Scribner, an imprint of Simon &
Schuster UK, Great Britain
Published in the United States by Farrar, Straus and Giroux
First American edition, 2003

Library of Congress Cataloging-in-Publication Data
Padilla Suárez, Ignacio, 1968–
    [Amphitryon. English]
    Shadow without a name / Ignacio Padilla ; translated by Peter Bush and Anne
McLean.— 1st American ed.
        p.   cm.
    ISBN 0-374-26190-3 (hc : alk. paper)
    I. Bush, Peter R., 1946–   II. McLean, Anne, 1962–   III. Title.

PQ7298.26.A285 A4713 2003
863'.64—dc21

                                                                    2002192529

www.fsgbooks.com

10 9 8 7 6 5 4 3 2 1

FOR LILI, CONSTANZA AND JORGE,

INTEGRAL TO MY INFINITY

I feel I am no one, only a shadow
Of a terrifying face I cannot see
And like the icy dark I exist nowhere.

FERNANDO PESSOA

CONTENTS

I

SHADOW WITHOUT A NAME

Franz T. Kretzschmar

Buenos Aires, 1957

My father used to say his name was Viktor Kretzschmar. He was a pointsman on the Munich–Salzburg line and not the type to decide, on the spur of the moment, to commit a crime. His apparent rashness in adversity concealed an extremely calculating mind, an ability to wait years for the right circumstances to hit a long-cherished target. So, while apparently taciturn, he was privately given to unforeseeable outbursts of rage, which made him a time bomb on a short fuse. These were not spontaneous impulses, but the product of that endless soliloquy he pursued with his defeated self, as one who, I'm sure, could have drilled a tunnel through basalt rock driven by the hope of one day recovering the light which was snatched from him in his youth. I once saw him hide for more than ten hours awaiting the reappearance of a famished hare which had dodged his first shots of the day. It was night-time before the animal finally surrendered to its executioner, finished off with a flurry of kicks which soon reduced it to an inedible lump of blood and snow.

Years later, while my father half-heartedly denied the railway tribunal's accusations, I asked my mother if she remembered that story of the hare, but she could not or would not answer me. Since the accident she'd locked herself into an impenetrable silence in solidarity, I thought at first, with the family's disgrace. Later, however, when she heard the judge's verdict, my mother sighed deeply, dropped her head and let out a wail of relief, freed at last of a burden that had poisoned every second of her existence. My words of consolation, offered from the depth of my own confusion, barely calmed her. Then, as if making an indirect reply to my question about the hare, she pointed at my father and muttered, 'That man, my son, is called Thadeus Dreyer, and he despises trains from the bottom of his heart.'

At first I thought my mother was delirious, referring to someone else – as if a perverse shadow had suddenly appeared behind Viktor Kretzschmar, the cause of all his misfortunes, and especially of the disaster that was likely to keep him in prison for the rest of his days. But my mother's gaze was unequivocally fixed on her husband's anxious face. She had decided to reveal to me the true nature of the actions and torments of pointsman Viktor Kretzschmar.

I'd known since I was a child that my father's real name wasn't Viktor Kretzschmar and it hadn't in the least sullied my blind admiration for him. For me, it had always been a closely guarded family secret, permeating my existence and giving rise to a boyish conspiratorial pride. On the other hand, this unexpected declaration of his hatred for trains had the frisson of a revelation which cut the cord between childhood and maturity. As far back as I could remember, I'd always thought my father had adored trains, ever since the day when, on board one, he'd staked his destiny on a game of chess and won. That someone could doubt the importance of a pointsman or the grandeur of those imposing metal beasts plunged him into endless depression. His eternal devotion to everything to do with railways had taken up his entire life; now I think his existence was, in some way, dedicated to demonstrating that his peculiar way of procuring the pointsman's job was more than an anecdotal whim of fate. He'd believed the game of chess on board a train heading for the eastern front in the war of 1914 was the culmination of a plan hatched by a compassionate demiurge, sparing him from certain death.

For a long time I'd imagined that historic game played in a sumptuous smokers' compartment packed with officers and high-society ladies. The gloved hands, swaying crests, ivory pieces and aromatic pipe-smoke flooded my childish fancies for years, and my parents never bothered to disabuse me. After the accident, however, I heard from my mother that things had happened quite differently.

My father must have been younger than I thought, though not young enough to avoid the 1916 levy that shook the outer rims of an Austro-Hungarian Empire intent on reinforcing its eastern front. Somewhere I still have a photo of my grandfather – a peasant from Vorarlberg about whom I know next to nothing – in the village station bidding farewell to the last of his uniformed offspring. The old man is wearing a satisfied smile, inconceivable in someone surrendering his son to a war which would soon be a lost cause. The young recruit doesn't seem to share his father's enthusiasm; he's looking the other way, his smile forced, wanly embracing my grandfather as if about to faint in the middle of the station. It's almost as if he's waiting for a chance to run out of the photograph and vanish into the mountains, where the whistle blast from the train about to carry him before the cannon of the Entente won't reach him. I reckon he's barely twenty, no more, and his face betrays the fear of a young man discovering, perhaps too late, the value of his short life which was suddenly under threat. I imagine my grandfather had to order him to smile for the camera and perhaps felt it necessary to push him towards the train with the unrelenting energy of an old peasant whose greatest satisfaction in life, according to my mother, had been to sacrifice his two eldest sons to the fatherland. Whatever the truth of that, the fact is my father didn't find the nerve to head for the mountains, and was left cowering in an old, dilapidated compartment, completely unlike the carriage of my fantasies. There he must have sunk into a moribund lethargy, his cadaverous hand waving goodbye to his family through the broken window which brought in an ominous gust of wind and the locomotive's infernal smoke. My young father must have sat there some four hours before his opponent, the real Viktor Kretzschmar, entered the coach.

I find it difficult to understand why I always imagined Kretzschmar to be an impeccable Victorian gentleman, maybe a retired officer whose mere presence would have instilled in the recruit a mixture of panic and respect. Perhaps my father once described him like that in his desire to hide the pathetic reality of the scene and its tragic consequences. Or perhaps it was simply the unruly engine of my imagination. Years later my mother cut that image down to size. The man on the train, she confessed, sobbing, as we left the courtroom, was just one more young man from the provinces who had contrived to use a distant uncle's influence to avoid conscription and get a job as a pointsman in the Salzburg district. Weaving her own fictions as a woman wounded by her husband's disgrace, my mother described this mysterious gambler as an alcoholic, a rabid opportunist who took a sick pleasure in snaring idle travellers and adolescents resigned enough to the disasters of war to gamble away their few possessions to a stranger. Of course, I don't know how far my mother's version had been skewed by my father's admissions during more than fifteen years of chequered matrimonial bliss. All in all, and I'm not sure why, when the accident happened and the judges suggested pointsman Kretzschmar's carelessness could well have been premeditated, my mother's description turned the Victorian gentleman into a terrifying spectre: suddenly, my glorious image of the real Viktor Kretzschmar was replaced by the striking vision of my youthful father shaking with fear, rushing to wrest from a drunken Mephistopheles the coins he hoped would cheer his last days in Belgrade.

My father, I must insist, was never the model of moderation. That night, to begin with, he was robbed of all he had in a couple of minutes. Unlike my mother, I don't think this happened in a game of chess; it seems more likely to have been a banal hand of poker played with marked cards or sleight of hand picked up in some low dive. Equally, I doubt my father was unduly worried by losing money he would have frittered away on Turkish cigarettes or Hungarian prostitutes. What must have driven him to see that contest through and transfer it to the chessboard, where he operated more skilfully, was some compelling need for at least one triumph before enemy artillery ended his journey in defeat. His rival must have spotted this desire for victory in the conscript's eyes. He perhaps also felt the moment had come to stake everything, not on a chance hand of cards, but on a game at which he was also expert, one much more worthy of the fearsome wager both travellers were about to place on the small table in that dingy compartment.

An adept chess player, my father used to say whenever he explained a masterly move to me, recognizes immediately, even in the strangest of circumstances, those who are his peers. However, he embarks on a game only when he is sure he has measured his opponent's strengths, and never – absolutely never – will he wager on the outcome anything less than his own life. I don't know which of the two made the initial proposal, or at what ill-starred moment the board eventually made an appearance. I do know the game's parameters were soon starkly defined, through the haze which clouds the rest of the story. If my father won, the other man would take his place on the eastern front and hand over his job as pointsman in hut nine on the Munich–Salzburg line. If, on the other hand, my father lost, he would shoot himself before the train reached its destination.

It may seem ridiculous, but that kind of suicidal wager was common currency in this time of tribulation when lives, minds and fates were particularly fragile, and the identity of a pointsman or recruit mattered little to the imperial authorities, provided the empty slot were filled. In a war which seemed infinitely protracted, sooner or later all men would bleed to death in the same trench. Their names, like their lives, would be levelled to an echoing anonymity. In my opinion, the wager never included (as my mother suggested in her eagerness to hide young Kretzschmar's sinfully suicidal impulses) a chimerical piggy-bank packed with gold coins which my grandmother was supposed to have given the last of her sons as a farewell present. I think it more likely that the money, if it ever existed, was lost in previous games. The idea that the man on the train was ready to gamble his life against his opponent's death is more in keeping with the almost sacred importance my father bestowed on chess and with the mental state he had been reduced to by a diabolical traveller intent on securing pacts in which the gambler faced certain defeat, when even a win would only prolong an evidently barren existence.

Unfortunately, my father didn't read it like that on the night. He preferred to use all his wiles to serve the reckless greed of one who for the first time has undreamed of treasure within his grasp. Time, I know, showed him the futility of his victory, but at that moment he must have felt his wager with the pointsman was a promise of immortality,

rather than the first hint of the painfully slow death awaiting him in hut nine on the Munich–Salzburg line.

The game can't have lasted long, for my father
exchanged identity documents with his opponent as the
train approached Vienna. As a reward for his chess-playing
prowess, he also received the real Viktor Kretzschmar's
railway uniform and the small chessboard on which he'd
staked his life and which afterwards he kept hidden in a
chest till the day he was sentenced. Now everything was
his, along with the life he had exchanged that night for
certain death under enemy fire – a death which, for his
own sake, he preferred to regard as utterly unavoidable
until a few days before the disaster.

My father faithfully carried out his duties as a pointsman
for over fifteen years. At first, no one noticed the least anxiety or slightest show of remorse which might have
betrayed his imposture and the relentless way someone
else's life was poisoning him body and soul, turning him
into a shadow. His unbounded enthusiasm for railways
was the mask he used to deceive almost everyone, except
my mother, a woman endowed with an uncommon and
painful intuition for less evident truths.

From the first day my father took great care to assume
his new identity fully. Hut nine was situated on the western

edge of the Salzburg region, an extremely busy crossing even in wartime. Given its importance, the post included a wooden cabin, vast in the eyes of someone like him who'd grown up in the proverbial penury of Vorarlberg. That cabin immediately became the home of the new Viktor Kretzschmar, native of Galicia, exempted from military service by a respiratory affliction which initially he tried to affect but which ended up conspicuous for its absence. Soon the inhabitants of the region got used to his presence and began calling him Viktor Kretzschmar, until finally even he was convinced the name was really his. His job only required absolute punctuality in the changing of points and the occasional dispatch to his superiors of reports which varied little in their detail. Having established a life of torpid routine, he was soon off to the villages near hut nine, searching for a wife to help him populate his cabin with what he hoped would be numerous offspring.

I don't think my grandparents ever completely understood that their son, who for them was still called Thadeus Dreyer, had traded his destiny so unexpectedly. Nevertheless, I'm sure that the old peasant in the photo, who'd surrendered him to the war, anticipating a third commemorative medal in return, never forgave him for renouncing self-sacrifice on the altars of the fatherland. My grandmother, for her part, wrote him a dozen or so letters in which, despite her absent son's insistence, she continued to call him Thadeus. Eventually, my father broke off the correspondence, completely consumed by his identity as pointsman Viktor Kretzschmar. He may have feared his mother's letters would expose him as a deserter, or perhaps he was worried that they would keep reminding him he was an impostor. And so he killed off the son the elderly couple insisted on reviving. They were unaware that, at the time, the man who answered to the name Thadeus Dreyer was almost certainly being killed on the eastern front, from where the news was more and more dispiriting.

But my father's total rejection of that name and past and his initial contentment weren't enough to prevent him becoming obsessed by this idea, which he must at first have considered trivial but which later took pride of place among his nightmares. While the war lasted, not a single day passed without the pointsman's going down to the city in search of confirmation of his own death. Surrounded in the early morning by potential widows and the grief-stricken elderly, he waited for the post office to publish its list of those fallen at the front. Every last trench of the great conflict was opened daily before him, yet the name Thadeus Dreyer never appeared – that arcane, unmentionable name my father never managed totally to destroy. Later perhaps, back in his cabin, he imagined receiving a letter from his parents, mystified by notification of the death of conscript Thadeus Dreyer, and asking for an explanation. This thought may have been some consolation to him, since he'd broken off contact with my grandparents who, after receiving this information which might well have failed to reach our post office, would at last have mourned his death, imagining a distant corpse, its features now erased by French shrapnel or Balkan worms.

Those dreams of self-slaughter must have given my father little relief, for he soon dedicated body and soul to legitimizing his new life through other means. I expect he fantasized with relish conceiving a hundred children who would spread his new name to the ends of the earth, but the wife he chose managed to bear him only one, a son. A son, moreover, who came too late; I was born in the last days of the war, after a series of miscarriages through which nature seemed to be reminding my father of the hateful masquerade of both his name and his body. Before my birth, the inhabitants of the area became used to seeing pointsman Kretzschmar's wife pregnant and childless. As a result, when at last one of those pregnancies concluded happily, the gossip-mongers had good reason to doubt that the son was legitimate.

Defeated thus by nature's obstacles to the perpetuation of his new identity, my father devoted his energies to convincing the world that destiny had meant him to be an exemplary railwayman. His monomania was worthy of better causes. Following the questionable premise that a man is no more than his work, Viktor Kretzschmar became the most zealous and best-informed pointsman of the nascent railway industry bequeathed us by the war. In addition to the point changes he executed every afternoon with ritual precision, my father papered the walls of his cabin with the innumerable diplomas the company awarded him year after year in recognition of his labours. Those papers said nothing that wasn't printed on the diplomas of his predecessors, but he exhibited them as if they were repeated acts of baptism, veritable documents of identity whereby his bosses blessed him in the eyes of the entire world with a kind of anointment by rail. As if that weren't enough, he patiently gathered together in hut nine a railway archive which served to complement his encyclopedic knowledge of everything related to his trade: diagrams of engines ancient and modern, postage stamps, daguerrotypes, crude engravings, extensive maps of railway networks in countries with unpronounceable names, and even a bunch of novels partly or wholly railway-themed, which my father read with that illiterate's moroseness he never entirely shed. All these things were the main furnishings of my childhood home. And they were also my playmates, my textbooks, the metal or paper phantoms that soon significantly reduced the space in our cabin as if Viktor Kretzschmar was thereby supplying the siblings I never had.

I don't know when our house became too small to store the material expression of my father's delirium. All he had collected and knew about the railways would have enabled him to graduate from Vienna as a first-class railway engineer, but he was content with the construction of a small annexe to our cabin. It was there my father built his own model of the world, a world of lurching trains whose inhabitants would never suspect their creator was a nameless, false demiurge. The clearest image I retain of him in those days is of his slightly bewildered look as he gazed at the model engines from London or Berlin, the peaceful villages he fashioned in pine, the tiny junction hut painted in the colours of the Austrian railways and inhabited by a lead hussar disguised as a pointsman. Evening after evening my father proudly operated his network, trying out innumerable point changes until he reached a perfection well beyond a child's grasp. I watched him with fascination, trying to forget that right then my mother was travelling to Salzburg to look for work, not always in a legal or honourable trade, to enable her to plug the gaps in our budget left by Viktor Kretzschmar's railway mania.

The accident happened in 1933, just after Hitler was elected chancellor of Germany. None of us saw or heard the trains collide because they did so some kilometres up the line from the hut, in a valley quite near the city of Salzburg. People summoned to testify at the railway tribunal nevertheless described the events, and with such precision that everything became unreal to me, as if the exact description of flames, destroyed carriages, corpses trapped amid red-hot metal, and wounded clamouring for help in the middle of the level ground had existed only in the witnesses' extravagant imaginations. During the hearing, my father had to listen to description after description while seated on a bench which made him seem smaller than he was, as though he had begun to change into the lead pointsman who up to then had presided over the correct running of his model trains. He had aged overnight, but his steady gaze and the close attention he paid to his accusers' diatribes betrayed not a flicker of guilt. He seemed preoccupied by something more important. It seemed that the fact of the disaster, to all appearances caused by his negligence, concerned him less than the secret motives that had given rise to it.

In one of the few exchanges we managed during the trial, my father asked me to bring him as quickly as possible a list of the names of those who'd died in the derailment. It wasn't easy. When I was eventually able to hand him one, I almost regretted I had. As he read the list of the victims, his face went deathly pale, and that pallor

17

stayed with him from then on. From his lips came curses on the world that were new to my ears. His eyes ran up and down the list hundreds of times in a furious rage, no doubt more furious than when, years ago, he'd looked for Thadeus Dreyer's name on the lists of those fallen in the theatre of war. At last, my father ripped the list to shreds as tiny as the pieces of his model railway, silently bade me farewell and waited with no great optimism for the tribunal's verdict.

Days later pointsman Viktor Kretzschmar was given a prison sentence for criminal negligence. I thought the gravest injustice in history was being committed, but something inside me suddenly hinted that my father was paying for a final, botched attempt to settle an ancient debt with the ghosts of his past. By then my mother had confessed to me in detail the real source of his name and job. There was no doubt that that exchange of identities effected years ago in a train heading for the eastern front was the motive behind the accident and justification for a sentence that could well have been harsher.

While I listened to my mother's despondent story, I remembered that the afternoon before the accident my father had gone to the city on the pretext of wanting to buy a catalogue of locomotives. He'd returned to the hut unexpectedly drunk and shut himself in the annexe with his model railways. Next morning, after locking the shed, he'd gone back to work, trying to hide a depression that lasted until the moment he went to attend to the points. During his calvary in court my father was adamant that a surprise attack of asthma – the result of a respiratory problem conveniently recorded in his identity papers – had prevented him reaching the points in time to change the lines. But, his argument carried little weight when it came to determining his responsibility for the disaster; I have to admit it hadn't convinced me or my mother.

Driven by my mother's revelations and the tribunal's verdict, I went back to the hut that afternoon and forced the lock. My suspicions were confirmed by what I discovered in his miniature railway universe. My father had rehearsed the catastrophe that would cost him his freedom and peace of mind. The locomotive and its carriages sprawled over the middle of the model; there were no flames or dead bodies, but their silent ruin invoked the disaster that, for the first and only time, Viktor Kretzschmar had managed to portray in real life. On the floor, wrapped round the tiny uniformed lead hussar of a pointsman, I found a scrap of newspaper announcing that Lieutenant Colonel Thadeus Dreyer, decorated with the Iron Cross for his heroic actions on the eastern front during the 1914 war, would be travelling the next day to Salzburg, where he would be a special guest at a meeting of the Austrian wing of the National Socialist Party. My father had at last found the man he'd sought for so many years, a man now enjoying a fate which wasn't his and which, I realized, only death could reunite with its first owner.

Two hours after my discovery in the annexe, my mother came home accompanied by someone who was to mark my life forever. That very morning his ample, disturbing figure had been among the spectators at the trial. He'd stayed to the last moment, waiting, with an ostentation worthy of an otherworldly judge, for the railway tribunal to deliver its verdict. My mother had also noticed him that morning, not fearfully, as one might register a stranger suddenly interfering in one's private tragedy, but like someone picking out an old acquaintance in the crowd. To judge from her level gaze, he was there by right, as if he were part of the convoluted process of judging Viktor Kretzschmar's crime.

For my part, the man's providential appearance in the courtroom was never enough to allay the suspicions stirred by his dress, his florid speech and the zeal he later showed in guiding the future of this prison orphan.

'Mr Goliadkin is an old family friend,' my mother lied as soon as I opened the cabin door to them. 'He'll help us keep afloat now your father's in disgrace.'

Still upset by my investigation of the annexe, I bleated a

tepid welcome, and was hard put to hide my surprise when our visitor held out his left hand to greet me.

'I lost an arm at Verdun,' he explained, grinning vaguely in an amused, mechanical response to my own awkward gesture.

My mother, meanwhile, was busy getting him a cup of coffee. For the moment she didn't seem ready to give me any further explanation or comment on the tribunal's verdict. Perhaps she thought Mr Goliadkin's mere entry into our new, bleak ignominy would be enough to end our life with the pointsman and usher us into a new existence. In a way, she was right: the short, chubby Mr Goliadkin had taken a seat and was laying a heap of banknotes on the table.

'I think,' he said eventually, 'the railway tribunal has today committed a huge injustice against Mr Kretzschmar. I hope, my boy, you'll accept this small gesture of support.'

His words were spoken with resignation rather than benevolence. It was as if his visit, his gift and even his compassion were reluctant, part of a ritual, the solemn payment of an ancient debt on behalf of a long-standing debtor. My mother must have sensed my doubts when she saw that I stood in the doorway as if turned to stone and didn't rush to accept Mr Goliadkin's offer.

'Take them,' came her unusually authoritative instruction, and she pointed to the notes our visitor had put on the table. 'That money belongs to us.'

With that she hastily thrust a cup of coffee in front of Mr Goliadkin's widowed hand.

I'd never seen my mother so flustered and yet, at the same time, so sure of what she was saying. From childhood I'd been used to the silences of a submissive woman abandoned by her husband for his mania. I felt that she wanted to blot out her life with pointsman Viktor Kretzschmar, and also that, for some strange reason, she was quite confident our visitor's money belonged to us. Neither then nor since did she bother to explain why, and I think she was right not to. After all, that was a part of their history only I could unravel; if it hadn't been for her discretion, this history would have fallen into oblivion the moment Mr Goliadkin mumbled an awkward invitation to look him up in Vienna if I ever passed that way, before shutting the cabin door behind him without tasting a single sip of his coffee.

After that night, I often accepted Mr Goliadkin's favours, but only rarely did I manage to strengthen the link I supposed ought to exist between a young man from the provinces and his generous benefactor. He soon adopted the disturbing habit of coming in and out of my life most opportunely – a brusque, sour intervention by someone carrying out a mission he found rather unpleasant. Such individuals are inevitably awkward in their dissimulations, palpably inept at camouflaging the calculation behind their actions, even when the latter appear charitable, if not heroic. From the start it was clear Mr Goliadkin hadn't placed those notes in front of me out of philanthropy, let alone for the friendship supposedly binding him to my unfortunate parents. At the same time I was certain my own thoughts about leaving that situation behind, which developed gradually after the unnerving inspection of my father's shed, were equally obscure to conventional morality. So I accepted help from my impure guardian angel and believed that, whatever the fount of his charity, divine justice had led him to me so that I might one day avenge the lost honour of pointsman Viktor Kretzschmar.

The first thing I managed to confirm after Goliadkin's visit and my father's imprisonment was that Lieutenant Colonel Thadeus Dreyer had cancelled his visit to Salzburg at the last minute. The newspapers said nothing about why he postponed his encounter with fate that day, but I was sure that sooner or later he would interpret it almost as a signal from on high. Who could blame him? After all, his escape from death could only be an unambiguous sign that God held in store for him a great destiny, a lofty mission which my father, the real Dreyer, could never have accomplished.

At first I was plunged into uncontrollable rage by the idea that Lieutenant Colonel Dreyer had these thoughts on receiving the news of the derailment and the subsequent sentencing of Viktor Kretzschmar. Later, however, I began to wonder whether my father's startling failure wasn't confirmation that, on occasion, fortune amends its errors of birth and reassigns to its offspring the name or destiny rightly theirs from the first day of creation.

I suppose my father also interpreted his defeat as divine confirmation of his own predestined mediocrity: from then on he renounced all attempts to ingratiate himself with the life he'd been dealt. The local prison became just the final casing for the being he now felt indefinitely chained to. If before the accident his face had revealed a flicker of anger fed by revenge, as the years passed he completely failed to see how he could reverse the past or the future. Abandoned by my mother, and perhaps overcome by the ghosts of those he'd caused to perish on the rails, he gradually fell into a heavy, torpid silence, his back bent almost to his waist. Isolated and diminished in this way, he didn't bat an eyelid when some time later I told him that, thanks to the good offices of his friend Mr Goliadkin, his name had appeared on a list of political prisoners given amnesty by the Nazi government.

That happened in the middle of 1937, only four years after the accident and the triumph of the Nazis in neighbouring Germany. Goliadkin announced my father's release in a cheerful telegram in which he also took the opportunity to repeat his invitation for me to visit him in the city, though it was Berlin now, where he foresaw a prosperous

24

career for me alongside certain individuals who expressed great interest in meeting me. At the time, I'd almost completely rejected the notion that my father's fate might be the punishment his mediocrity deserved, and had as a consequence renewed my sullen desire to pay Thadeus Dreyer back for his criminal survival. The physical and mental wreck that was pointsman Viktor Kretzschmar, forgotten even by himself in the darkness of his cell, had dug an enormous pit in my mind that was now draining all my reasoning, all my vital energies. So Mr Goliadkin's telegram, rather than placating me, came at the right moment to reaffirm my path. The providential release of the human ruin my father had become struck me as a cruel joke, a provocation by affluent people who, like Goliadkin or Dreyer himself, felt they still had the right to play with the destinies of those they'd humiliated. My occasional benefactor could use my father to satisfy his delusions of grandeur, but I wasn't prepared to submit my decisions to his sense of justice. It was his business if he insisted on helping us. And I'd make quite sure his help was only used to execute successfully the rebellion that at some stage my father had begun against men like Thadeus Dreyer.

I always knew it would not be easy to reach Dreyer, but I never imagined he would be protected by the very course of history. That year, as well as the major upheavals brought about by the Nazis' unexpected triumph, Berlin greeted the news that my father's old rival had been promoted to general and was, moreover, one of Marshal Goering's closest collaborators. Nobody could tell me with any certainty what his role in the Reich High Command was, but to judge by his erratic public appearances and the ambiguous nature of his appointments, he must have been directing one of those high-security projects with which Goering won the Führer's trust. Some officers I met through Mr Goliadkin spoke of Dreyer evasively, as if he were a powerful but resented superior, an Austrian upstart whose influence on Marshal Goering and even on the Führer himself was inexplicable. Goliadkin claimed, like many businessmen of the time, that his own relationship with the Nazis was restricted to economic rather than political connections. And so, he said, he was sorry he couldn't help me with an investigation which he anyway considered eccentric and unjustified.

'If you're so interested in the military,' he suggested unenthusiastically in one of the few conversations I managed to have with him on the subject, 'I recommend you enlist in the army immediately and join the party as soon as possible.'

The suggestion wasn't entirely foolish, and it was obvious my benefactor had the means to launch me on a successful military career. His office was always packed with young men from the provinces who, like me, were waiting for that patron of German youth to indicate that they should don their best attire and repair forthwith to the lair of some officer too burdened by debt to refuse the protégés of powerful Mr Goliadkin. Curiously, I never again bumped into those anxious youths, but I was sure our benefactor had placed them at the heart of the Reich with a display of authority suited to men who take pleasure in pulling the strings of other people's lives.

Even so, initially I followed Mr Goliadkin's advice only in part. At the time I had nothing but contempt for the military. Besides, the atmosphere was quite hostile to an Austrian citizen and, perhaps, the army was too slow in moving people through the ranks ever to allow me access to General Dreyer. In the end I only joined the National Socialist Party youth movement, hoping another way would soon present itself.

Years later I understood that in fact it would have made no difference if I'd begun my military career with the Reich. I say this not just because of the obvious truth that any career in that nation inevitably became militarized, but because General Thadeus Dreyer, transforming himself from persecuted to persecutor, would have found me sooner rather than later. My confrontation with him was not a question of time and did not depend on decisions I might take in exercising my illusory freedom. Unbeknownst to me, over those years I was restricted to wandering a labyrinth whose gates opened or closed before me and led exactly where others wanted me to go. I enjoyed all the freedom of a brutalized laboratory rat running around a maddening model of the cosmos.

My days in the Reich, spent in a brilliant progression through the College of Railway Engineers, sped by at the dizzy rate characteristic of the era. I always sought access to General Dreyer when the opportunity presented itself, but sometimes I forgot that this motive should have guided my every act. There was nothing so futile in Berlin as a personal motive, whatever it might be. Even individual memories eventually dissolved into the huge miasma of a common, grandiose future in which men need no longer worry about their petty gripes, let alone the legitimacy of a name that would evaporate in the enthusiasm of happy, anonymous multitudes. Such a vision could blind anyone, but sometimes, when I was being dazzled in the middle of a meeting or a parade, my secret reasons for being there – alien and even opposed to the party that sheltered me – demanded a painful return to common sense or the particular, ravaged memory of my father. I would then return home, my stomach churning, or drown myself in drinking bouts, doing little to repair the damage wrought on me and so many others by the relentless struggle between an exultant mass and each individual soul.

I'd like to think it was chess that partly spared me from descent into madness or a pistol shot to the temple which would have curtailed my days of waiting in Berlin. Many years had gone by since my last chess lesson from my father, but I soon discovered I still had the resources necessary to mount a sound defence and now found pleasure in a game which had hitherto left me completely cold. Overnight I realized that my initial faltering efforts had only been a consequence of the violence with which I'd been taught. Viktor Kretzschmar's mania had filtered into his lessons and made me think that the secrets of the game to which he gave so much importance had been denied me at birth. Now, though, chess gave me a chance to exercise my battered reason and keep a tight rein on an identity which daily threatened to splinter into fragments amid the excited crowd. When I faced the chessboard even Dreyer's spectre seemed harmless: the entire world paraded before me as if, momentarily at least, I no longer existed among men and could act like a solitary god whose freedom was as infinite as the ways to put a king into check.

Curiously, nobody waxed more enthusiastic than Goliadkin about my return to this arcane territory. He usually received the other decisions and accidents in my life with indifference, almost as footnotes to a drama he knew by heart. In the case of chess, his interest was so exaggerated that I felt uncomfortable. As soon as I began to frequent clubs and tournaments, Mr Goliadkin decided to become a punctilious witness of my defeats and victories. He inevitably turned up in clubrooms the moment a game was about to start and stayed there, silently attentive as at my father's trial, noting down each of my moves with his left hand, nodding approvingly at each of my declarations of check or hiding a grimace when he contemplated the fall of my queen. It was obvious my benefactor knew little of the secrets of the game, other than the most rudimentary of its rules. Nevertheless, he followed my progress with the delight of an amateur. And though he'd leave before I could greet him, he always left me feeling the game had been staged exclusively for his benefit.

After several months my game had progressed enormously, and I even boasted there wasn't a single chess master in Berlin who hadn't conceded to my attacks at least once.

'All except one,' said Mr Goliadkin on hearing of my claim, and added that, if I wanted, he could arrange for me to join Reinhard Heydrich's chess club, where the keenest, most skilled member was Thadeus Dreyer.

That was enough to bring me abruptly back to reality. Until then, Goliadkin had showed no sign of knowing the secret motives that had previously led me to ask after Dreyer. But there was no doubt now he'd known all along. Moreover, he'd listened to me patiently, as if, in addition to any ties to my father, he had reason enough to wait for the right moment to engineer a meeting that might end not, as pointsman Viktor Kretzschmar would have wished, in vulgar murder, but in a game of chess.

That day I felt towards the enigmatic Mr Goliadkin a respect and admiration bordering on friendship. I felt suddenly bound to him by a common project to cast General Thadeus Dreyer into ignominy. Whatever his reasons for wanting to humiliate the man, he could now rely on me to help him achieve his goal. We had common objectives. It was he who'd first understood that my revenge was to be not glorious regicide, but the total public destruction of my enemy, in a similar confrontation to that which, in other times, had enabled him to usurp my father's fate.

My warmth for Goliadkin was short-lived however. One night soon after, I discovered that not even he had been the legitimate master of my destiny. This flash of insight came from a chance encounter, of the kind that studs the existence of men like my father and myself fated not to steer the course of their own lives.

In a small Berlin suburb, where I wound up on one of my rowdy binges with the Hitler Youth, I suddenly found myself abandoned by my companions in a truly lugubrious dive. Outside, a murky, relentless rain poured down, and I thought it better to wait for the alcohol to settle than to risk disappearing like so many old soaks whom the Berlin dawn found frozen stiff beside some sewer. I vaguely remember the place was an outsize matchbox, a bar just like any other I used to visit on student sorties. A smell of beer and cheap make-up hung in the air, over a patchwork of solitudes draped across a counter where, by that hour of the night, they served only watered-down liquor. I was marooned, a shipwrecked sailor who hours earlier thought he'd been hoisted into the crow's nest of a brigantine and didn't now know when or why his vessel had met its end.

Suddenly, through the window I saw two silhouettes pass by, stop on the nearby street corner and engage in leisurely conversation, indifferent to the rain lashing down. The shadows stopped me distinguishing anything but their outline, which had a military air and made me think of two officers engaged in secret, if not subversive, plotting. I was moved by a curiosity I didn't understand to abandon the den and approach them. One was turned away from me, strong and straight-backed like a Viking, while the other, shorter and barrel-shaped, hung on his words like an underling. The latter's hazy features, the few of his words I managed to catch, and his servile gestures dredged up a memory, first murky, then suddenly stark and clear: the man was none other than Mr Goliadkin. Even today I can remember the disquiet the encounter produced in my semi-stewed brain. In other circumstances I would have rushed to thank my benefactor yet again for his countless favours, and perhaps taken advantage of the chance to ask for an introduction to his companion, clearly from his appearance an important member of the Third Reich's army. But something about those drenched, furtive shadows stopped me approaching. A vague intuition, one of those moments of lucidity which sometimes sear the mind like lightning, told me that chance had led me to Mr Goliadkin that night not so I could overwhelm him with gratitude, but to teach me that nothing in life is as gratuitous as we like to think.

In fact, almost before I had managed to place Goliadkin he must have sensed my presence just a few steps away. The unexpected interruption, a slight gesture to his companion, made the latter look over his shoulder and allowed me a glimpse of the damp brow, the sharp, prematurely aged features of General Thadeus Dreyer. I know neither of them could have recognized me in the gloom of night, yet my intervention in their clandestine dialogue must have spread a panic in them equal to if not greater than that which they'd caused me. Perhaps thinking I was one of the numerous spies who lurked in the streets of Berlin at the time, they buried their faces in the collars of their overcoats and strode hurriedly off into the darkness.

The first thing I wondered about as I made my way home was how Mr Goliadkin had ended up in Dreyer's clutches. How absurd that the manipulators of two apparently distinct threads in my existence could come together and appear in the same scene. If Mr Goliadkin was merely an instrument wielded by the usurper of my father's destiny, each of my successes was nothing but a humiliating, unacceptable affirmation of Dreyer's guilt. Or, worse, perhaps my benefactor's suggestion that I should challenge Dreyer to a game of chess rather than kill him might have been an artful way of rendering his boss's potential murderer into a mere boastful, rancorous youth. For the boy would surely stop pestering him after a crushing defeat at the hands of the general, for whom this second humiliation of the Kretzschmars would confirm that the gift of his name and heroic destiny came from the gods.

To think, on the other hand, that the relationship between Dreyer and Goliadkin was a chance affair, completely independent of the ebb and flow of my career, was a no more reassuring alternative. A few days later I realized it was not even the unexpected sight of those two opposites which was really at the heart of my anxiety, it was the vague recognition that the vision of Dreyer's face, which I had seen before only in blurred photos or at mass meetings, had stirred within me. From that encounter on a Berlin night, I took away the vision of a face whose lines had suddenly seemed too familiar, too suspect. I had seen that profile (a little less sallow), that slightly squinting gaze, that hair now greying, hundreds of times in the mirror. General Thadeus Dreyer's features were presented to me as an insistent, deadening portrait of my own future – not the one my father would have wanted for me but that which we all carry inscribed in us from conception, a destiny to endure to the last day of our lives.

Perhaps the idea that Dreyer might be my father was at first too chilling for me to stamp with the seal of certainty. Time, nevertheless, was to give it that currency, though whether as a damning or a saving grace I have yet to discover.

Our troops invaded Poland in the autumn of 1939. War had revisited the continent, and events unravelled frantically, as if it were all happening now for the first and only time in history. A frenzy of marches, banners and metal masked the ashen spectacle of thousands of men heading in unison to sacrifice. The Austrian contingent of the Reich's army brimmed with exuberance, and I cannot deny that I let myself be swept along with the tide, forgetting for a moment how much I loathed it all.

After the botched encounter in the Berlin suburbs, I had been able to confirm that my benefactor was in fact a faithful orderly of General Thadeus Dreyer. Apparently, the two men had met and fought together on the disastrous Balkan front during the Great War, and ever since then Goliadkin had remained by the side of the man who had returned from the front to receive the Iron Cross my father always thought was rightfully his. So there was no doubt that Dreyer knew of my existence, or even thought it practically belonged to him, as my father's had. I was, I confess, quick to hate him for this brazen appropriation of my destiny, but in the months between that discovery and the occupation of Poland I was unnerved by a feeling of loss, a strident clash of emotions which in the end convinced me that Dreyer regretted his imposture and had resolved to salvage the Viktor Kretzschmar debacle in his own way. Once again, it was a crude, facile idea, a petty self-justification to avoid pushing my desire for revenge to its ultimate conclusion. However, at a time when everything seemed on course for a feverish descent into the abyss, that conviction made more bearable the void which threatened to strip me of the last hold I had on life. This transformation being wrought in my soul eventually expressed itself in deeds which slowly revealed a certain

36

despair, a grey blur of indecision, apparently designed to confirm in the eyes of the world that, despite my suspicion that Dreyer was more than my enemy or protector, I really deserved rather to be the son of defeated pointsman Viktor Kretzschmar.

My mother had died of syphilis some five years before, so suddenly that I didn't have time to get to her funeral. My father, for his part, was wasting away in a Frankfurt sanatorium, unable to recognize me, let alone appreciate my shaky efforts to restore his peace of mind, which was lost forever. In such circumstances, a fatal confrontation with Thadeus Dreyer would have been not a mere settling of accounts with his father's substitute by Viktor Kretzschmar's son, but a self-immolation which would have redeemed the pointsman's disintegration. But, in fact, my fleeting encounter with the general and his orderly stripped away any desire for reproach. Hatred, the driving force determining every one of my acts in recent years, was suddenly replaced by total indifference to men and events; it seemed that the only thing left to me was to seek out in Poland the certain demise which had once awaited Viktor Kretzschmar on the eastern front. I felt it my duty to join this new war, hoping a patient sniper, hidden in the dense Slavic woods, would shoot me down and spit on my corpse. It was the only way left for me to take from Thadeus Dreyer some control over the life he had built for himself with Goliadkin's help, as well as an existence he'd rejected years ago in a train heading for the eastern trenches. To have been contemplating a game of chess against Dreyer now seemed almost frivolous, an absurd enterprise from which I would emerge the loser, whatever the result. My death – specifically my stupid, cowardly death in a war I didn't believe in – was the only way to make Dreyer account for each of his infamies.

My father's impersonator, nevertheless, must have glimpsed the trajectory of my suicidal logic, for he contrived to steal a march on the black offices of death. Even today I like to think my second encounter with Dreyer was not as fortuitous as he initially tried to make it appear. And though sometimes I suspect it was destiny and not his or Goliadkin's machinations that brought us together, I think by that point I considered any little twist of fate, however strange, as marked with the name of Thadeus Dreyer.

A few weeks after the Reich's troops were finally settled in Poland, I was sent to the front with a group of technical auxiliaries to the occupying forces. For over three months, ignorant of the reasons behind it, I had collaborated closely on the design of a large-scale railway map of the German–Polish frontier, contributing, as I later discovered, to the decisive success of the Führer's first major military offensive. Now I was required to devote myself to the unpleasant task of establishing bases from which the lines could be reconstructed, and used to move materials and prisoners to the forced labour camps our troops had begun to build in Poland. I should have realized that those duties, set out with such bureaucratic sterility in my mobilization order, concealed the ominous fire of blood lust which had apparently taken hold among us since the signing of the Treaty of Versailles in 1919, but actually, whether I channelled my knowledge of railways towards this or that objective was a matter of complete indifference to me. Individual faces, names, destinies were by then so submerged in the anonymity of armed multitudes that it would have been pointless to pretend the whirlpool of history could be calmed by the opinions of individuals flailing in its chaotic eddies. I felt the war was above all intended to emphasize my inability to free myself from my father's shadow and escape from a template on which my fate had already been imprinted.

But destiny is a wilier opponent, keeping us alert – sometimes our enemies make occasional feints to stop us surrendering to passivity, or, perhaps for a moment, we are lulled into the belief we can also pull some strings to guide our future. I was taught that lesson in 1941, during my stay in Poland. Everything was practically ready for Operation Barbarossa, and I was awaiting the order from my superiors to swap my engineer's compass for a rifle. A friend who had got on in the party, and was now working as a photographer for the German High Command, had invited me to witness the progress of the Treblinka prison camp. I accepted, delighted to be released from my interminable wait to go to the front, a suspended state of nervous tension very similar to that of a man under sentence of death who longs for dawn and the climb to the scaffold. In just over two hours an armoured train would take us to the camp on tracks I had helped design, and there the Treblinka Commandant would welcome us with a gathering full of orgiastic promise.

That is how, aided by the privileges attaching to my recent promotion to lieutenant, I finally came to enter a sumptuous smokers' carriage packed with ladies in gloves and officers of high social standing. But far from enchanting me, that scene brought to life from my long-forgotten childhood fantasies reared up like the most terrifying nightmare. I remember the sticky heat, so at odds with the winter which had already spread over the Polish territory as if trumpeting the catastrophe which would soon befall our troops at Stalingrad. By my side, my friend grimly cleaned his camera lenses.

Suddenly, a roar of laughter drew our attention to the back of the carriage. A huge officer in full dress uniform was making his way towards us. Tall, fairly broad-shouldered, with the confidence of a war veteran, in the midday light General Dreyer possessed the unmistakable if unexceptional nobility of one whose every gesture was controlled by an iron discipline. As he made his way through the other passengers, his stature grew. Mr Goliadkin stumbled behind him, smiling at me, half gleeful, half embarrassed by what was about to take place. They reached us at last, as if they'd swum through an ocean of seaweed. Dreyer greeted me with a familiarity which must have seemed excessive even to Mr Goliadkin.

'Greetings, my dear Engineer. I've wanted to meet you for such a long time. My orderly has told me so much about you' – and he sat down opposite me without waiting for a reply. He quietly ordered my travelling companion and Mr Goliadkin to go and drink to our health, as he had unfinished business to settle with me.

Once we were alone, General Dreyer expressed his pleasure at the opportunity to talk to an Austrian on such a Prussian journey. Oblivious to my indifference, he took off his uniform jacket, stayed silent for a few moments, then said, 'Kretzschmar . . . In the war of 1914 I knew a pointsman from Galicia by that name. An excellent chess player, to be sure.'

The very cordiality of those words galled me. Dreyer pronounced his vowels in that strange, neutral way characteristic of men who have spent too long in too many parts of the world, citizens of that phantom province which stretches from Finland to Trieste. As he spoke, he spread his huge hands over the table, almost as if preparing to play a pastoral overture on an imaginary piano, for an audience of one. The mere mention of my father felt at once offensive and unnecessary. For a moment I wanted to demand that he reveal his intentions once and for all, but I was restrained by the intuition that these ironic opening moves were a necessary part of the small sacrificial ritual we had both engaged in.

'My father, General,' I lied with the only truth I could offer my interlocutor, 'was not from Galicia but from Vorarlberg.'

Dreyer looked mildly surprised but unperturbed, and then smiled as if he understood my sarcasm, replying that he had also been born in the south-east of Austria, although he regretted not remembering any Kretzschmars there.

'Perhaps,' I responded, thinking it was the way to end the foolish exchange, 'it's because my father left the region when he was quite young. Towards the end of the war he started working as a pointsman on the Munich–Salzburg line.'

General Dreyer's smile broadened into an affable chortle which disappeared in the smoke of a cigarette he'd just lit.

'Oh, Salzburg,' he replied as if daydreaming. 'A magnificent place, Engineer. The most beautiful women of the Empire flourished there by the dozen. You're too young to

42

know this, but at the end of the war it became an obligatory port of call for us soldiers.'

I felt the whole world turning upside down in my head. The shadow of Thadeus Dreyer had entered my spirit like a furious demon, blinding me even to whether or not his words were the confirmation I'd feared of my own illegitimacy. I was gripped by the idea that, just as he'd arranged my father's release from prison, he might well have overseen every stage of my life and helped me at every step. I wanted to stand beside him right then in front of a mirror and trace each one of our features – those same features my father must have seen reflected in me year in, year out. Every event in my life became an aspect of a plan controlled by a faraway brain: the money my mother brought home from Salzburg while my father spent his wages on his railway mania; my father's release, my own rapid rise through the ranks of the National Socialist Party; the ease with which I finished my engineering studies – all conformed to the strict laws of the conspiracy Thadeus Dreyer, assisted by Goliadkin, must have plotted against my father or perhaps against himself. And I felt rage, a paralysing rage directed not at the general but at myself, at my inability to blame him for anything, rage at my startling gratitude for what he was now suggesting: that my entire good fortune, and perhaps my existence, had been given to me by a man who had achieved what my father, stigmatized by mediocrity, never could. Rage, too, for the memory of my mother, whom Viktor Kretzschmar's mediocrity had brought low, made pregnant year after year, suffering the contempt of being dispatched to God knows what obscure streets of the city in search of sustenance and the disease that had killed her. I don't think any man in my position would have been able to bring order to such emotional turmoil. I doubt I managed to hide my embarrassment, and thought I recognized what might have been a crude wink of recognition, as though my interlocutor had also been waiting for years, to send his son, biological or not, into this necessary, if not obligatory, state of chaos.

A few seconds must have passed between General Dreyer's words and my superhuman effort to recover a degree of composure. The train which had emerged from my childhood daydreams chugged on towards Treblinka, full of smoke and officers oblivious of the conversation between a fledgling railway engineer and an old soldier. We would soon reach the Nagosewo tunnel, where I could quite easily take advantage of the darkness to shoot Thadeus Dreyer. But the circumstances now seemed to have arranged themselves very differently, not actively preventing my plans but rendering me unable to fathom why I'd pursued this confrontation for so long. The only thing I could think to do was draw from my briefcase the small, battered chessboard I had found some years before among my father's possessions. The general affected a smile at its appearance and echoed the terms of a wager he or my father set all those years ago: if he defeated me I must submit myself entirely to his designs. If I won, he would blow his brains out before we reached Treblinka.

'Anyway, you know, sir,' he said, setting out the pieces on the board and smiling paternally, 'I like to lay bets where both sides come out winners.'

As the train drew close to the Nagosewo tunnel, I merely nodded again and replaced one of my pawns with the small lead hussar that Viktor Kretzschmar had once draped in the colours of his pointsman's threadbare uniform.

II

FROM SHADOW TO NAME

Richard Schley

Geneva, 1948

W hen I first saw him, stepping down from the train with the rest of the reinforcements from the Ukrainian front, I naturally had no way of knowing that Jacob Efrussi, my old playmate from the poverty-stricken outskirts of Vienna, had changed his name to Thadeus Dreyer. It's true that in October 1918 the Austrian front in the Balkans was beginning to turn into pandemonium, in which the most sensible thing to do was to give up one's name along with everything else that made up a condemned man's identity. That afternoon, however, I was still a long way from appreciating the blessings of anonymity in the middle of war. I suppose that's why I took heart at the appearance of a familiar face among the thousands of blurred features I'd seen descend on

49

Belgrade station over the last weeks, en route to the Serbian trenches.

Less than a month before, Father Ignatz Wagram, stationed there to provide the consolations of religion to our troops in the Balkans, had returned to my seminary in search of a novice to assist him in his gruelling work. He delivered his exhortation during vespers, although it was immediately clear his words were directed exclusively at me. I was, after all, something like his spiritual son, and it seemed only logical I should be ready to follow him to what he regarded as a worthy culmination of any life consecrated to the service of the dispossessed. Father Wagram had an idiosyncratic sense of the priesthood and would sometimes speak of ordination as a second birth, a sort of new baptism, for which a novice must be entirely stripped of his past in order to acquire his definitive identity. No memory, no aftertaste, should mark the chosen's mental tabula rasa if their desire was one day to anoint their souls with the indelible holy oil of the priesthood. Often this conviction led Father Wagram to treat me extremely harshly, but I knew that his underlying intention was always to have me follow the path of those wandering souls who are suddenly offered the chance to redeem themselves through martyrdom. As soon as I saw him enter the seminary chapel, with his black badge and two stars embroidered on his cassock, I believed I understood how far the limits of his faith would carry him. So I had no choice but to volunteer to be his aide on that suicide mission, which I also thought of as a golden opportunity to make myself someone in a war in which not only men but whole nations were doing their utmost to become nothing or no one.

All in all, two weeks in the Karanschebesch camp on the banks of the Danube had been enough to make me seriously doubt the wisdom of my decision. Shortly after he reached the trenches, Father Wagram was killed in the field, in the middle of saying Mass, by a mortar shell which reduced him and the altar to a pile of blood-streaked cloth. A few days later, someone painted this sarcastic epitaph on his gravestone:

> You were surprised to get what we had coming.
> You promised us the Kingdom of Heaven
> But the sky fell down on your head.
> Where once you bellowed, now rest your bones.

At my insistence, the Captain General's office assigned Staff Sergeant Alikoshka Goliadkin of the duty office to uncover the perpetrators of the sacrilegious ditty. But no one, not even the most devout officers, seemed remotely to care about the results of the investigation, which was eventually consigned to oblivion. As for the Viennese

Curia, they displayed a marked lack of interest in replacing the murdered priest, and I was soon spending my time denying last rites or collecting, from the most unlikely sources, hosts consecrated by some reticent, renegade priest. The late Father Wagram had once managed to wrest away my past on the altars of our faith; now his absence flung me into the arms of a second, more desolate abandonment, as vulnerable as an orphan. I soon realized that Father Wagram had been mistaken in believing the priesthood could bring out the true man, for a cassock can just as well dilute our identity by hurling us into the most flagrant impersonations. Utter uncertainty and a corrosive emptiness began to gnaw at my spirit like a malignant cancer, and in that company I eventually came around to the idea of carrying out ecclesiastical functions authorized solely by the silence of my superiors. It was the devil's task to convince a dying soldier that my status as lowly seminarist did not allow me to hear his confession or administer the holy oils, and so, painfully, I grew accustomed to performing the priestly duties I had once thought sacred, and to leaning my head ambiguously to one side when a delirious, blood-drenched recruit called me by the dead priest's name.

So my eagerness to get through the crowd to reach my friend Jacob Efrussi at Belgrade station that afternoon must have seemed manic, as though a lunatic had imagined himself in the middle of the ocean and begun flailing for the piece of wood which would save him. My friendship with Efrussi certainly hadn't been without its quarrels and dramatic partings, but right then I thought of him as a brother – that other person in whom we recognize ourselves and who we imagine keeps safe our lost memories. I clearly remember his name sticking in my throat a couple of times before I shouted it over the heads of the rest of the recruits. And I remember equally with bitter astonishment his reaction to my shipwrecked plea. Efrussi stopped as if he'd been shot in the back, slowly turned his head and faced me for a few seconds; I thought I saw the brief glimmer of the smile of someone recognizing scattered fragments of his own memory in the face of another. But that light, whether it was real or imagined in the rush of my enthusiasm, was quickly replaced by a furious glare and soon swallowed up by the crowd.

I spent the hours after my thwarted reunion in the Karanschebesch duty office searching for Jacob Efrussi's name in the lists of troops recently drafted to the front. I knew the field surgeons would, as usual, be clamouring for my miracle-working in their improvised wards of dying soldiers. But that afternoon I didn't feel up to the task of replacing the morphine they preferred to sell on the black market in Belgrade. If the doctors needed a priest, they could invent another one – they had done it with me and it would be easy enough to replicate my blasphemous fraud with one of their own. They would just need to learn a couple of Latin tags and use their bloody bandages as prayer-scarves; the soldiers *in articulo mortis* would never discover the deception. Anyone could give a blessing, and obviously in this war one didn't need ordination to listen to boys who mechanically intoned their sins with the precision of those who haven't lived long enough to be guilty of anything.

My scrutiny of the list of new arrivals proved fruitless, and only helped confirm the impression that Jacob Efrussi's presence in the Balkans was a mistake or a hallucination. I didn't even quite know what I was doing at the duty office myself. It began to feel like a simple evasion of my intolerable ecclesiastic responsibilities. Who, after all, was Jacob Efrussi? My scant memories of him only surfaced when I saw his face in Belgrade station, and now didn't seem much different from those of any other of my friends from Vienna. Why, then, was I behaving as if Efrussi had concealed in his cartridge-belt a message as vital as the one dying soldiers demanded of me to explain what had brought them to be slaughtered in the Balkans for the sake of the Austro-Hungarian Empire? As I continued to read through the names of the recruits, those questions drummed in my brain, abrasive and insistent. Time and again the name Efrussi led me to search those childhood memories which had survived Father Wagram's labours for something that would assuage my fears that this ghost was only another assault on my sanity. I kept seeing Efrussi jump over a fence or awkwardly head a battered football, and then suddenly identified him with a dark stairway leading to his father's jewellery shop. Once or twice I conjured a memory of his being chased by a gang of angry adolescents; another time he was the one hounding a group of smaller, frightened children among whom I could make out my own face, deformed by the weak light of the compound's lanterns. The images of Jacob Efrussi raced through my brain with nightmarish logic – they were far from what childhood memories ought to be, particularly those of a childhood that I, in the seminary, had nostalgically thought of as a rather tranquil period in my life. There was something archetypal and artificial about those visions, something rather blurred. They were only meaningless fragments, ectoplasm of memory that offered little of the support my disturbed state craved.

When the lists of recruits began to assume the same bewildering chaos as my memories, I decided: damn it all to hell. And I would probably have sent myself to chase it if Staff Sergeant Goliadkin had not burst into the duty office, returning from one of his frequent sorties to the camp bar, to give me, at least in part, the certainty I'd been seeking. Despite his failure to identify the desecrator of Father Wagram's tomb, I bore him no grudge. In my opinion, Goliadkin was inoffensive enough, although, from another perspective, he deserved more respect than any other man at Karanschebesch. Inevitably mistrusted, as were all the Cossacks who had recently joined the imperial troops, despite the loss of his right arm at Verdun, the staff sergeant's good offices and legendary ability to wield a sabre with his remaining hand had allowed him to stay in the army, as if war were the only world where he truly existed. He was one of those many individuals who, for a couple of beers, offer undoubted talent for violating the basic threshold of what, in other circumstances, is considered legal. Far better-equipped than most to cope with widely varied situations, he was incapable of displaying good manners in front of his equals, and faced his superiors with a flattering respect which lasted only as long as it brought him some benefit. I always found his company at the front heartening, for his elemental drive to transgress put me at my ease – I was sure he felt the same about my 'priestly' rank as he would have about a sergeant who had attained his by seducing a general's wife.

That afternoon, Goliadkin must have noticed something inside me was amiss, for his slurred greeting swiftly took on an unusual tone, somewhere between cloying and paternal. 'Greetings, Pater. Why don't you go and get a bit of fresh air? You look dead.'

He immediately collapsed on the desk laughing as if parodying a grotesque death to make his point. I left him to it for a while until I decided to ask him if by any chance he remembered the name Jacob Efrussi among the new arrivals at the camp. The staff sergeant lifted his chin, looked at me in silence, and then, in one of those rare moments of lucidity that descend on hardened drinkers, answered, 'Efrussi? I don't know the name, but I can assure you, you'll not find him here. Everyone knows Jews always manage to avoid conscription, or at least to get assigned to a post in the rearguard.'

Far from disappointing me, the sergeant's words were immensely soothing. Suddenly, that gloomy staircase I remembered leading to the jeweller's acquired a rare luminosity, and I could see two boys preparing to begin a game on a well-worn chessboard. I could almost feel again the vague, long-forgotten elation I'd felt when the jeweller's son agreed to share the secrets of that game of kings. Gradually the image grew very sharp, as did the furious calls of my father, who interrupted our match that afternoon to drag me home and ban me from ever risking humiliation on the chessboard at the hands of the son of a usurious Jew.

From this memory I was sure it would not be difficult for me to recover many more: the corpulent Jacob Efrussi torn out of my life with a violence that must have seemed inexplicable then, perhaps so wounding that it took me some effort to forget it. As Goliadkin had reminded me, the possibility of locating a Jew in the Karanschebesch camp, or anywhere else in an army where Jewish soldiers were conspicuously absent, seemed less likely than ever, but at least his spectre had brought back a piece of my childhood precise enough that it could be the first strand which would unravel a skein of memories I'd once considered lost. And so, overwhelmed by the possibility of encountering not Efrussi but my own disjointed memory, I thanked a perplexed Goliadkin for his valuable information and left the duty office.

I don't know how I managed that afternoon to avoid the doctors' demands that I attend to their dying patients. Perhaps for a few hours at least, death interrupted its tireless reaping so I could abandon myself to the pleasure of chasing the whirlwind of memories gathering in my brain with dazzling coherence. Back in my hut, which I'd formerly shared with Father Wagram, I took off my cassock and lay down on my own bunk for the first time since my protector's death. My head ached so much that at any other time I would have gone straight to the infirmary, but the pain now seemed slight compared to the storm in my heart. I meditated on the surprises the unchained beast of memory might hold in store. I thought of Efrussi, of the loneliness of boys isolated by their fathers' designs. I could almost hear him dragging his feet on the way to synagogue, as if the mere idea of flaunting his Jewishness through the streets of Vienna was an unbearable weight upon him. I also conjured up his innumerable precocious chess victories, always gained under the watchful eye of his father, who strove to turn those childhood victories into public demonstrations of the superiority of his people. More than a game for the jeweller, chess was the indisputable proof of a collective identity of genius, bred in his son across millennia of persecution, diasporas and fearful defence of a racial consciousness maintained through pain and blood.

Later I thought of my own shortcomings as a chess player, my plodding inability to frustrate, even once, Jacob Efrussi's victories. Like him, I spent many afternoons playing under my father's instructions, and frequently had to pay for the humiliations which the jeweller's son indiscriminately dealt out to the city's young Lutheran and Catholic chess players. I suddenly realized I had never understood my father's determination to isolate me from the freedoms of childhood and teach me chess by flogging me, yet at the same time keep me away from another boy who seemed likewise condemned to be the instrument of an abhorrent traffic in honour and identity. Even if I couldn't remember it clearly, there was no doubt in my mind that Efrussi and I had been set against each other several times, not on the stairway to the jeweller's but in that Sunday salon where Herr Isaac Efrussi promised to write off the debts of the father of whoever proved capable of beating young Jacob at chess. My public defeats at Efrussi's hands, therefore, would have meant not only racial or religious humiliation for my father, but the loss of a substantial sum of money which he, more given to drinking than pride, owed to the jeweller's dubious generosity.

Along with these memories came the disgust of knowing I'd been little more than an animal unsuccessfully trained to fight another over a debt incurred in beer halls and brothels. Despite Father Wagram's efforts at erasure, that state of mind didn't seem at all alien, as if those images had been consigned to a corner of my brain but were never fully extinguished. I recognized the apprehension in my memory of the jeweller's stairway perfectly well, and as I've said, started a chain reaction of memories, reaching past the war and my brutalizing stay in the seminary, to a self-awareness I'd suppressed. I could attach forgotten scenes of domestic violence to the inflamed voice of my father, before he was killed in a bar-room brawl shortly after I entered the seminary. There were lengthy chess lessons and strategies I had to practise against myself alone in my room, open-air winter punishments in Vienna's alleyways, nights full of yelling and threats which ended with me huddled in bed defenceless against hell fire plagued with Catholic traitors, Jewish usurers and Ottoman infidels. Those wretched scenes most probably occurred after the frustrated game of chess on the stairway, maybe the only match Efrussi and I had actually wanted to play, free from the deplorable bet the jeweller thrust on those challenging his invincible offspring. It was also likely that those scenes were a daily occurrence until I ran away from home to take refuge in the seminary. I didn't believe the Catholic faith offered genuine liberation from my father's intemperate Lutheranism, but in desperation turned to that Church as solid ground on which to stand against his determination to destroy my conscience.

It was now easy to understand why my substitution for Father Wagram weighed so heavily upon me, and how much I resented him for putting me in the position of a false priest. The blessings I gave to the young men heading for the trenches must have been far from heartening; my words, my gestures and even my presence could only have told those poor wretches of my unease at my imposture and my rapidly dwindling faith. I imagined that, once dead, the ghosts of those soldiers would discover my fraud and haunt me forever from some shadowland beyond the Danube, as if they had also been cast into icy non-existence by a drunken fanatic of a parent. That I wasn't responsible for the circumstances leading to my imposture was far from soothing, but at least now I could say I was fully aware of my situation again. I owed such clarity to the recruit I had seen in Belgrade station, whatever his name may be. I had found the real Jacob Efrussi in my memory, and, given that the chances of a young Jew finding his way to the south-eastern front were in those days extremely remote, I spent my time bound up alone with my own ravings instead of searching the camp for that shadow torn from the body that gave it life. If that body were to be found in Karanschebesch, I incanted to myself until I fell asleep, my destiny would let me know in its own good time.

My chance to meet the recruit from the station came sooner than I'd expected, just a few days after my visit to the duty office. And I must admit that, in the circumstances, the encounter was less mortifying than I'd initially feared.

That afternoon Staff Sergeant Goliadkin came running to the priest's quarters to warn me that truckloads of wounded were on their way back from the front. As was to be expected, an officer of the Queen Olivia regiment soon demanded my presence to hear the confession of a lieutenant wounded on the Piave, where the Italians had our troops in serious trouble. The regiment's surgeons had already amputated the poor man's legs, and he was now surrendering the last of his healthy flesh to the relentless advance of gangrene.

The scene played out like any other: the lieutenant's sweaty hands clasping mine, his mouth unable to articulate the enormity of his sins, his eyes appealing for a peace I couldn't grant. What now made me feel especially uncomfortable was the idea that even the doctors and officers blindly accepted my imposture, as if they'd also resigned themselves to accepting the solace offered by a seminarist falsely elevated to the priesthood. They'd stopped wondering how it was possible to count on so young a chaplain; they didn't even seem to remember Father Wagram. On several occasions I'd written to the Curia, no longer requesting but demanding the dispatch of a proper priest who would know how to fulfil the duties the war imposed, but the only addition my superiors made to their silence was the weight of an old cassock sent through the post, for my attention. Make good use of it, the bishop should have added while packing his bags to flee to Holland, and may God bless you.

After confessing the lieutenant, I had a desperate need to get drunk. The merest whiff of beer usually left me choked with nauseating memories, but that night I wanted to merge my affliction with the general grief reigning over the camp. Maybe I even hoped to cause a scandal and force the Curia's hand finally to replace me. In any case, I soon found myself wandering the camp in search not of Jacob Efrussi but of Staff Sergeant Goliadkin and it was he who took me to the Gypsies to buy a gallon of the badly brewed beer they sold to those who had enough money to drown the taste of impending death by the glassful.

I can't remember how much we drank. Night had fallen over the camp, escorted by those swathes of mist with which the Russian winds announce the proximity of winter and defeat. The full moon struggled to break through the darkness, adding its anaemic glow to the benzine lanterns that shone dimly on small knots of soldiers here and there. We must have wandered for almost an hour through that limbo of fake fireflies. The tents, the long lance-like shadows, and even Goliadkin's unusually silent figure, suffused my soul with a quiet, almost healing melancholy. Broken only by a sigh or chuckle from the staff sergeant, the silence added to the resigned air of impending catastrophe. We went into one of the supply tents. I took in tables and an improvised bar, and a number of soldiers gathered with the subdued bluster that accompanies last orders before curfew. None of them, when they saw me, showed the usual deference to my cassock. I imagined the spirits had granted me that night the long-coveted gift of invisibility. The soldiers didn't even look at us as we drained our glasses. Absorbed in his own lurid depression, Goliadkin muttered to himself in Ukrainian and Russian. It was evident that he, too, was reserving judgement and farewell laments for the defeat advancing in the deluge of cannon and gunfire which already shook the mountains across the Danube.

Suddenly, I found myself alone in my drunken state, walking down a narrow corridor between two long tents, desperate to empty my stomach, until I stumbled upon a group of men apparently deeply absorbed in a card game. A lantern lit the scene, forming an amber aura around the unmistakable profile of Jacob Efrussi. He looked a little different from when I had seen him through the morning mist at Belgrade station. His head was covered by a nondescript black cap, and his whole body wrapped in an officer's greatcoat with the insignia torn off. In the lantern-light his high cheekbones and sunken cheeks were even more pronounced. Seated at a table made of ammunition crates, his body radiated a damaged strength which fitted the clandestine atmosphere perfectly. As I approached, I glimpsed a trace of panic in his face, quickly replaced by the expression of someone immersed in a game not going as well as he would like. Leaning over the crates he resembled some kind of Titan bowed down with the weight of the stars and planets. There was something remote about the sight of him and his companions and I was quite surprised they didn't instantly vanish from my sight like any other bad dream. As soon as I saw them I began to leave, so as not to risk breaking a code I didn't yet understand, but checked myself when I spotted a small, all-too-familiar chessboard on top of the crates. Then, perhaps emboldened by the alcohol, I felt entitled to approach and call Efrussi by his name. The player stood up, hesitating for an instant like someone peering through the jungle for the beast whose growls have just awoken him. He walked over to me and grabbed me by the cassock, his eyes mere inches from my face. Finally I felt his breath, as liquor-laden as my own, if not more so, scorch my brow and say in a dubious High German accent: 'My name, Father, is Thadeus Dreyer. If you ever call me anything else, I swear I'll spare the French the bother of putting you out of your misery.'

The other players must have muttered something about my fictitious priesthood, for they quickly immersed themselves in the game again. Meanwhile Goliadkin emerged from the shadows, mumbling drunken apologies in my ear with the fervour of someone who has just witnessed a sacrilege. I let him go on as if he didn't exist, and walked away from the players much less offended than I might have expected. Efrussi's threat had disguised an imploring tone, a conviction less violent than his words. Although I couldn't yet fully articulate it, I knew that conviction related to me. The man had seen in me something which gave him a vague certainty, almost a premonition, which was leading him to defer the inevitable recognition. I had only to wait. Efrussi would take care of the rest.

Expecting destiny would pursue its course, I spent the following days observing conscript Thadeus Dreyer, trying to see past the steely deadpan of his face, to the secrets only I could decipher. I soon ascertained that my friend, despite his efforts to the contrary, had barely changed over the years. Since adolescence, Efrussi had been one of those men condemned to resemble only themselves. In his case, the singularity of his physical appearance had to be a kind of stigma, underlying the many ways he tried to hide his real features. Words and gestures he must have stolen from someone else did not succeed in disguising his central being. Those tapered, angular features even seemed to tire of the perpetual mutation Efrussi insisted on inflicting on them. The gaunt but harmonious profile of his forebears inevitably surfaced, as if all those centuries of diasporas and migrations had scarred him as the wind carves a channel in granite. Efrussi, in short, could not fool me with his supposedly Prussian beard, the occasional curl in which – despite what must have been hours in front of the mirror – always betrayed him.

Moved by sympathetic curiosity, or perhaps the desire to profit from the situation should the opportunity arise, Staff Sergeant Goliadkin had offered to help me track Efrussi down. It was he who verified that, at least according to his identity documents, the man was actually called Thadeus Dreyer, said to be a native of a village in Vorarlberg, who had soon become known in Karanschebesch as invincible in games of chance, as well as chess, whose ancient code of honour he stained by betting his challengers vast amounts of money. More than once, Goliadkin informed me, officers of his regiment had demanded that my old playmate adhere to regulations that still reigned in the camp, but Dreyer had always escaped serious reprimand. His money, he lied in self-defence, was sent to his parents in Vorarlberg. And since chess, unlike cards or dice, was not proscribed in the army, the authorities really had nothing to reproach him with. To all this conscript Efrussi added that he could beat anyone who cared to challenge him in whatever circumstances, and rumour had it that some officers fond of the diabolical game were so indebted to him that they could no longer impose punishment.

All this information, imparted by Goliadkin during long, boozy chats conducted at my expense, led me to believe Efrussi would surely know how to use his influence to keep himself safe in the rearguard. To my surprise, however, I soon found I was mistaken: in October that year his regiment was summoned to the trenches, and Efrussi, to my consternation, was going with them. Even Goliadkin felt betrayed by this, as if the fact that Efrussi had not, in those times bereft of heroism, taken advantage of his power to save himself was a grave offence against the most elemental laws of what he, in his idiosyncratic code of dishonour, considered right. Whatever the case, we both watched as Efrussi crossed the Karanschebesch bridge radiating a satisfaction in contrast with the feeling of doom which oppressed the rest of the soldiers. One might even say the recruit had been looking forward to this moment, as if the bloodletting awaiting him on the other side of the Danube was the supreme tournament whose highest, lethal prize was his by rights.

The French cavalry devastated Efrussi's regiment almost immediately, and his contingent scattered in the Serbian mountains before anyone reported for certain how many soldiers had fallen in the ambush and how many had sought refuge among the enemy troops. Days later Staff Sergeant Goliadkin announced that if I wanted more accurate news of Dreyer I could get it first-hand from a sergeant who had arrived that morning from the trenches. For an instant, judging by the unpleasant look in the poor devil's eyes, I thought he hadn't even recognized the name Dreyer, and that Efrussi had once again switched identities to evade my final efforts to recognize him. The sergeant, however, soon disabused me: 'That leech Thadeus Dreyer,' he muttered, 'must have died in the Beljanica valley. Or, at least, finally gone completely mad up there.'

Perhaps my friend, the sergeant added, was among the group of soldiers who had refused to abandon the trenches in a display of bravery which would have seemed rash under any other circumstances; on the decimated Balkan front it was frankly stupid. As far as I could gather from my informant's halting story, Efrussi's regiment had begun to retreat the moment the last of their commanding officers died in hand-to-hand combat. No one, in that case, could accuse them of desertion, but conscript Dreyer and his companions had stayed somewhere in the mountains, announcing they would not move from there until they received express orders to abandon the fight. The sergeant concluded that our companion in arms must now be in the hands of the French or, more likely, bleeding out his foolishness beside the rest of his suicidal regiment.

When I told Staff Sergeant Goliadkin the story, he agreed with the sergeant that Efrussi's gesture was pathetic. At that time terrible news was reaching us from everywhere: Kaiser Wilhelm II had fled to Holland, our troops were being ruthlessly devastated, and the French would soon be sweeping down on Belgrade. To add to that, it was said that at any moment the Uhlan, Ukrainian and Polish contingent among our troops, which were quartered in the towns of Karanschebesch and Eormenberg, would rise in rebellion and refuse to cross the bridge over the Danube. Nerves were more frayed than ever, and it was no longer possible to tell whether the danger threatening us would come from Field Marshal d'Esperey's troops or our own. If Efrussi really wanted to continue to serve what remained of the Austro-Hungarian Empire, he ought to have abandoned the trenches and rejoined a new, recomposed army which would enable him to give his life more fruitfully. I suspected, however, that his apparently foolish attitude owed nothing to heroism or to zeal to serve an empire subject to a code of honour as absurd as the war. That Efrussi had gone mad was evident from the start; it was the most obvious way to explain his actions.

But not even that theory finally convinced me. There had to be another reason why Efrussi had decided to stay up there. Perhaps, I thought, this was that celestial message my friend's phantom presence in Belgrade had heralded, and with that idea I resolved to take the first opportunity to find him. Maybe, I said to Staff Sergeant Goliadkin, I too was being called upon to commit an act of foolhardiness. Nothing seemed more natural than to launch myself into what by then seemed the last place on earth, in search of Efrussi, or my own death.

Events came to bear out my decision. As fears of mutiny mounted in Karanschebesch, and just when I thought the Vienna Curia had finally resigned itself to a campaign chaplain ordained merely by divine indifference, I learned that a new, legitimate priest would arrive on the next train. Goliadkin received the news anxiously, and was hardly surprised when I told him I wasn't going to wait for my relief to arrive. As soon as I heard the news I went to my superiors asking for authorization to carry the order of retreat to the soldiers in the mountains. As he signed the document, the officer I'd approached looked at me with the eyes of one who had seen too many absurdities in too short a time. I held his gaze: the Curia's message had restored not my identity but my anonymity so that no one, least of all me, could have given a damn whether I chased death by just walking out of the camp or by insisting on saving a band of lunatic soldiers. Towards the end of October that year the eastern front had finally dissolved into absolute chaos, the Empire's rearguard was crumbling and desertion alternated with the most breathtaking heroism.

'You go, Schley,' the officer said, having already forgotten my high ecclesiastical functions. 'Do what you like, and if you find any of those men alive, tell them from me they're a bunch of imbeciles.' And he dismissed me from the tent with the gesture of one who'd just signed a stranger's death warrant.

The journey to find Jacob Efrussi was beset by so many nightmarish experiences that I preferred for a long time to forget them. I can now barely recall the enormous difficulty I had in persuading Goliadkin to help me reach the Serbian side of the Danube. Along with the order of retreat I carried a safe-conduct the staff sergeant had expedited for me, in exchange for a case of unconsecrated wine, to get past the checkpoints. I never had to use it: one after the other, the control posts appeared before me unmanned, desolate as a stormy sea at night. The stench of mustard gas, mud and excrement ate into my spirit in such a way that even today I find it difficult to get rid of. Since then the entire world has been immersed in that distinctive, bitter odour, as if my sense of smell is condemned to perceive everything through the pestilence of death.

On the outskirts of Nic, the mule Goliadkin had managed to get me on the black market collapsed in exhaustion. Entirely alone in the field of battle, I circled around combat zones on foot. The wind picked up as I drew nearer the frontline. When I started along the paths leading towards the south-east, the gale lashed at me with sustained fury. The ravages of retreat began to appear: trenches filled with corpses from both sides, all dumped in an enormous pile at the bottom of those wounds in the earth, blending with the mud which, once again, reeked foul and Stygian. I spent a long time in the combat zone, a landscape I hadn't confronted since the death of Father Wagram. At some point in my descent into the Beljanica valley, where I hoped to find Efrussi, I exchanged a few words with two or three recruits who'd lagged behind, either out of loyalty or for the chance to loot their comrades' bodies. Once I also came across a band of Gypsies plundering what they could before the vultures swooped. In their eyes I saw the cold indifference of the starving, of beings designed to survive not through Goliadkin's cynical guile but by being reduced to the most brutal animality. I feared being hit by a mortar, or collapsing through exhaustion, as those Gypsies would strip me of all I had, unable to distinguish me from the corpses. No one was waiting for me in Vienna – no one had ever waited for me – and the things I carried in my cartridge-belt could hardly be considered of any worth. Nevertheless, they were all I had to give me the will to live. Next to my heart, Efrussi's order adhered to my passport with the same binding force that carried me forward. To lose those documents to Gypsy hands or death itself would have exiled my soul to a world of ashes.

That tortuous journey, which in other circumstances would have barely taken a morning, lasted several days. I travelled for a distance in a medical corps van, in which a couple of orderlies, in an echo of my own situation, acted as if they were the most highly qualified surgeons.

'What're you looking for up there?' one of them asked when he heard my destination. 'There's nothing but corpses left.'

When I explained I was carrying an order to relieve of their duties a group of soldiers from the disappeared Fourth Division, the orderly stared at me in astonishment. 'If it's death you're after, you could have saved us all this bother.' And he abandoned me in the middle of the road, as if unwilling to burn petrol to aid such a fool's errand. I don't blame him. He had a point, and I started to realize that the order to withdraw mattered much less to me than finding Efrussi or his spectre. I was on a one-way journey towards my sole point of contact with my past. I yearned only to be recognized, accepted by my old companion; the rest was incidental. I wanted to shout Efrussi's name for a final time and him to shout mine. That and that alone made me want him still to be alive and kept me going.

When I think about this and remember the devastated landscape of the Balkans, I'm convinced that only a benevolent deity could have arranged things to enable me to reach Efrussi. Today chances of such a marvel strike me as practically nil, and I feel as though I reached that accursed plain protected against enemy shells by a divine shield. Years later, I discovered that the valley where Efrussi's regiment had disappeared had by then been recorded for some time as territory conquered by the enemy. Then, however, that immense grass lake seemed to be a no man's land, a kind of untouchable valley of Jehoshaphat. If my information was correct, Efrussi and his comrades had to be nearby, in one of the trenches where the Gypsies had yet to loot the corpses. The hand-to-hand combat must have been gory in the extreme – for there wasn't a single place where the bodies of our men did not alternate with others bearing enemy insignia. The vista was so distressing that I was convinced I'd arrived too late. Still, a sort of ancient terror, like the trace of a tattoo, kept compelling me from trench to trench until, in the last light of the afternoon, I made out an abandoned-looking cabin on top of the hill. The building looked deserted but there was something about it that suggested the presence of a living hand. At first I didn't know what it was, but as I got closer I discovered the corpses had been lined up as though to lie in peace on top of this mountain of flesh swarming with flies. It was an awesome spectacle which revealed a hidden order, as if those allied and enemy corpses – an impartial plurality only death can grant but which perfectly summed up my image of the empire in flames – had been arranged so I myself would identify them or, maybe, join them. As I approached the cabin the corpses spread out before me like a trail of pebbles guiding a child homewards.

The cabin door was open. A barely audible voice answered my knock: 'Come in, Father.'

There was Jacob Efrussi, his back to me, sitting at a table covered in papers, the nature of which I couldn't make out. He was shaking, absorbed in a meticulous operation which prevented him from turning round. His hair had grown and almost covered his neck, giving him a lycanthropic air. The walls of the cabin, riddled with the unmistakable marks of gunfire, admitted the smell of putrefaction. Without looking up, Efrussi pointed me towards a chair on the other side of the room. I brought it over to the table and sat down facing him, searching out his desperate eyes above his hermit's beard.

I waited for him to finish his labours with the little hypodermic needle which he had been preparing when I arrived. He held it in his left hand and thrust it into his arm. His body was shaking so much that I was surprised he'd been able to find a vein. The morphine took a few seconds to take effect. His grimace gradually evolved into a beatific smile. When he at last managed to speak, his voice had a benevolent, velvety timbre.

'Morphine, Father, is the only sensible way to keep yourself together in this place. Unfortunately we haven't got much left, and it doesn't look as if you've come to bring us a new supply.'

Efrussi gave a wryly defenceless tone to his words, as if secretly hoping I'd contradict him. Time, hunger or the morphine had reduced him to a shadow, but that human wreck still held, perhaps even in spite of itself, a degree of vitality. I let a few moments pass before answering, my desire to speak hampered by my inability to think how to address him. I had waited so long for this encounter that now, before this bestialized image of my childhood friend, I felt as if I, too, had lost a large slice of my humanity. Efrussi, meanwhile, had retreated into demented contemplation of the papers covering the table. He smiled, talking to himself as though reciting an ancient prayer learned in the delirious world of his manias and terrors. When I drew close enough almost to brush against his face, I discovered it was a litany of names, hundreds of names, which Efrussi was reading from passports in front of him, almost all of them bloodstained.

When I could no longer bear my friend's whispering silence, I extracted the order from my cartridge-belt and handed it to him saying, 'You can go home, Jacob Efrussi. I've brought your orders to withdraw.'

Efrussi broke off his incantation and regarded the document as if looking through it. 'Efrussi?' he asked after anxiously reviewing the passports. 'We don't have a Jacob Efrussi.' And he threw the order on the ground. A wave of rage surged within me, not because I thought Efrussi was in any condition to recognize the value of the document, but because he persisted in denying his own name and, in so doing, denying me, dragging me into the anonymity of his madness, towards a point from which neither he nor I could ever return.

I jumped to my feet, grabbed his head and forced him to look at me. 'Who are you? Which of these is your name?' I shouted, pointing at the passports.

But Efrussi answered only, 'My name is Legion, for we are many.'

Hours later night enveloped the cabin and the countryside. Moonlight filtered in between the boards and found us still sitting at the table. Outside, the gale from the east clashed with the sound of explosions reverberating through the voiceless silence, as if they were wandering bolts of lightning, resigned to never touching the earth. Efrussi had recovered partial lucidity and mumbled an explanation directed not at me but at his imaginary judge, who doubt-less knew each detail of his drama perfectly but needed a confession to comply with an obscure, otherworldly con-tract. Suddenly the wind carried a blast of putrefaction to us, bringing Efrussi back to reality. 'One gets used to this, Father,' he said, breathing in the smell like a sea breeze. 'It's the perfume of death the leveller' – and he took a second breath with a shudder like the desire for morphine. My hopes raised by that small expression of sanity, I suggested that the best way to get his drug would be to return to the Karanschebesch camp. My friend did not greet the idea with much enthusiasm; he seemed almost offended by my mundane reasoning. He needed morphine, he commented, only when certain ideas, certain memories gathered from all the men he had been, overwhelmed his mind, provoking the devil's own migraine. For the moment, he added, those memories were more or less in order and he begged me not to ask him about them, as I wanted to. He simply wasn't going back, he'd spent his entire life in search of this place and this death.

'I have been everyone and no one,' he said with the sorrow of repentance. 'I have stolen so many names and so many lives that even you couldn't count them. The last one belonged to a poor recruit from Vorarlberg called Thadeus Dreyer. I traded my death for the name Viktor Kretzschmar and a miserable future as a pointsman. So you see, Father,

80

how little this soul you are so intent on saving is worth by now.'

Despite these words and Efrussi's obvious desire to die, I tried to dissuade him, saying that from then on he wouldn't have to steal lives, for we would both go back to Austria together, where we would forget all about the war. He thanked me with a smile intended to be warm despite the renewed trembling under his beard. His resistance to returning would be difficult to surmount, and I had started to realize his motives for being there. Efrussi was not mad. Rather, he was thinking with the crushing logic of the defeated, with the final resignation of a man who had been forced continually to flee an identity which had always seemed to him too onerous and confining to endure. In some way, in the past we'd both wanted to escape our condition, our race and the faith of our fathers, and now was the time to confront the futility of that flight.

Efrussi was not the kind of man to surrender to his death without a fight – although he'd been hinting at something of the sort from the start, I simply wasn't prepared to lose my only hope of redemption. Before, when I saw him in Belgrade, I could hardly have guessed the truth, but now it was clear I'd decided to define my whole being by the only person I'd ever wanted to be. It mattered little that Efrussi was now a crucible of souls, a congregation of fleshless names. Perhaps he didn't need me, but I would teach him to.

It crossed my mind that the way to force Efrussi to accept the proposal which mattered to me alone must lie in one last game of chess. Waiting for a liberating order which would never arrive, he had bet his life against each of his regimental comrades, so now he could have no objection to placing his last bet with me. The idea would have been outrageous in any other circumstances, but right then it seemed to fit the landscape before my eyes as much as did this grotesque and vigilant Cerberus. If Efrussi had waited for me, it must have been because he also wondered how that game my father broke up in our childhood would have ended. Now the terms of the game must be different. If Efrussi beat me, I'd present him with my corpse and my passport to keep him company in his grotesque Eden, until a stray bullet put an end to his suffering. On the other hand, if I won, Jacob Efrussi had to come back to Karanschebesch with me and submit to my desire to save his life in order to recover my own. Reluctantly, he agreed to my terms, and that night we resumed the game on our childhood chessboard.

Years later, during a brief trip through the Balkans, I calculated I'd walked about ten kilometres with Efrussi's body over my shoulder. At the time, however, it seemed much further. I remember the firmament, no longer obscured by fog, stretching above us in all its glory, boasting of its greatness as if it wanted to exacerbate my fatigue and the horrible sensation of carrying not one man but the dying bodies and souls of all the men Efrussi had been or could have been. The troops of the Entente had closed the high road to Karanschebesch by then, so I went into the woods and took the risk of being run through with a bayonet. Efrussi's body was extremely heavy, and sometimes it seemed he'd stopped breathing. Then I'd halt for a moment, call him by his name and receive a moaned reply, which only reminded me of my guilt at snatching him away from death.

At first I didn't understand why Efrussi had betrayed me like that, much less why it was I who now felt treacherous. I'd gone to impossible lengths to save him. I'd risked everything to return him to the world. Only the desire to keep intact my last link to the past kept me going. Nevertheless, as my hopes of reaching a first-aid post faded, I began to comprehend that Efrussi hadn't deceived me after all. I should have known my companion had resolved never to return home long before our encounter in the cabin in Beljanica. When he agreed to stake his fate on a game of chess, it wasn't a submission to my selfish enthusiasm to save us both. He wanted to show me that something had snapped within him, something which had kept him alive to that day and something from which the encounter with me had forever liberated him.

What had happened hours earlier came back to me as, on the point of collapse, I crossed the wood. Efrussi, I thought, must truly hate me for preventing him from committing suicide, from peacefully killing himself and passing the burden of his memory, his name and the indefatigable conscience of his race on to me for ever. To facilitate that, however, I had to beat him at chess. It was shortly before dawn. At no time did Efrussi show signs of weakness or resignation; he defended himself on the chessboard as if he truly desired my defeat. The match lasted several hours, the only sounds being distant cannon fire and the silent testimony of his dead. No furious voice or inebriated hand dragged us away from our game this time. We both seemed to be looking for a way to extend the game infinitely, as if only the path rather than the inevitable destination could bring us the pleasure we had so cherished. My concern that a lack of morphine would quench my opponent's spirit vanished at once: Efrussi played with the concentration evident in masters who risk their fate on every game, even when playing against themselves.

Dawn had almost broken when Efrussi's king came under threat. He contemplated the board for a few seconds, toppled his king and congratulated me, calling me

Richard for the first time. Then, as if nothing had happened, he suggested we sleep for a while, for the journey before us would be even more arduous than the one I'd undertaken to find him. I want to believe there was a trace of resignation which I, flustered by my victory, hadn't noticed. As I slept, somehow his breathing became part of my dreams and at some point, transformed into a vague intuition, led me to open my eyes. I saw Efrussi, his back to me again, putting a pistol to his temple. I don't think I have ever in my life felt so alert, granted that quickness of reaction of those whose lives are in immediate danger. At the very instant Efrussi pulled the trigger, I managed to strike his arm aside, though not far enough to prevent the bullet from blowing apart most of the right side of his forehead. Efrussi looked at me for an instant in dismay and then mumbled, as he fell to the floor, 'That was uncalled for, Richard.' And he slipped into that blood-soaked unconsciousness which lasted all the way to Karanschebesch.

Not far from the Danube I tripped and dropped Efrussi, who continued to breathe, as if the fall was just another part of the torment he had endured for years. His head bled profusely and he clearly wouldn't live much longer. At that moment I'd have liked to hate him, to confirm he could hear me from within that physical agony ill-suited to a man like Efrussi. All my premonitions came flooding back as I again hoisted him onto my shoulders. Some

85

corner of my conscience had begun a brutal metamorphosis: Efrussi, I at last understood, was prolonging his life in the hope that I would adopt his soul's logic and accept not only his death but the crushing weight of his race as well, the responsibility in the endless battle that he had not wanted or been able to fight, but that I, moved more by love for his ghost than by mere philanthropy, would now be obliged to take up in his name.

By the time we approached the camp, Efrussi had begun to let go of his life. I could feel it in the increased weight of his body, in the once deep breathing now reduced to the occasional shallow gasp, almost begging me to allow him to go. It was then that I reconciled myself to accepting his legacy and his curse. In Karanschebesch, where the enemy's cavalry helmets now alternated with the cheers of a legion of deserters, I went immediately to the duty office. As I had expected, Staff Sergeant Goliadkin was still there, searching through his innumerable folders for information that might be of some value in the world's chaotic future. Immersed in his sea of papers, he was a caricature of Efrussi reading the passports of the dead. Seeing me, the sergeant stood up, startled. He calmed down slightly when I laid Efrussi's body on the floor and he could begin to discern my features beneath the blood which caked my face. 'Is that you, Father?' he asked, his widowed hand swaying above his cartridge-belt.

'My name is Thadeus Dreyer,' I answered firmly, emptying before him the savings box full of money I had found among Efrussi's belongings.

Then, and only then, did I notice my friend's body relax for eternity, as if, freed from a legion of demons, he'd at last embraced the healing anonymity of death.

III

THE SHADOW OF A MAN

Alikoshka Goliadkin

Cruseilles, France, 1960

From a distance, General Thadeus Dreyer's house looked like a prison barracks transformed by the passage of time into a dark, mist-shrouded castle amid the streets of Geneva. Its walls stood in dramatic contrast to the snow's evening glitter, and light glinted from the upper windows as in the eyes of a giant cat surprised in the shadows by the torches of a reconnaissance patrol. As I paid the taxi driver, I felt the building had been watching me from afar. Everything about that scene – the demolished garden wall, the leaden snow on the rooftops, the amber of twilight so like dawn – seemed abruptly and painfully familiar. More than forty years before in the Ukraine I'd seen snow like this and crossed a similar enclosure with an agility given only to the young and the fearful. That day, next to a huge, abandoned estate, two freezing-cold men waited for me to take a shot – not under the cover of night or at some old man awaiting his assassin by a window, but in the full light of day, and into the heart of my brother Pyotr, an officer in the Tsar's palace guard. That morning, I remember, I had thought the imminent destruction of a man a necessary, if absurd, rite, and had also felt an urgent need to perform it before my stomach turned and I vomited into the snow.

I didn't bother to search for my keys to let myself into the house. I knew Dreyer wouldn't have wasted his energy locking up, not because he thought it unnecessary, but to indicate that he was expecting me, and perhaps that deep down his ravaged soul had sensed what fate held in store. From the moment I pushed open the door there was something offensive about the predictability of my movements, as if the sacrifice had been rehearsed so often in my dreams that it had been stripped of all meaning. Every object in the mansion gave off an air of almost festive indifference. The sofas where we reminisced and dozed during the war years, the seemingly interminable dining-room table, the chessboards, the coats of arms along the walls of the corridors, all welcomed me, bluff and familiar, like someone who has long prepared for the visit of a friend he barely recognizes. I was about to call out, wanting only to break the hospitable silence, when the house itself changed my immutable course. Suddenly, as I approached the stairs, I caught a scent of something which, in other circumstances, I'd have recognized immediately as gunpowder. However, afraid that Dreyer might have anticipated my plans, I preferred to put it down to a pipe or to that untamed memory of the Russian dawn when my brother fired his shot with a barely concealed grimace of contempt.

The afternoon before, Pyotr and I and our seconds had agreed that the duel should be at ten paces, but on the day my brother's face, his Tsarist palace-guard insignia and his fur coat seemed as distant as the shapes in a swiftly fading dream. Pyotr had chosen his finest clothes for the occasion of his twin brother's execution, and shaved off his beard, emphasizing the differences between us that had ruled our lives and in the end led us to that place. Seeing him appear on the hillside, I imagined the long hours he must have spent in front of a mirror, thinking not of dying or even killing me, but imagining a photographer hidden in the thickets who wanted to immortalize his glorious moment as an angel of death. Perhaps in that way, I thought while our seconds took an age to examine our weapons, Pyotr hoped the eternalized moment of my death would pass from hand to hand until his atamans greeted it with cries of approval, dispatching him back to St Petersburg and rescuing him from obscurity. It would be his reward for avenging my drunken insults to Cossacks like himself who stayed stupidly faithful to Mother Russia, denying that we were and always had been a stateless race of mercenaries.

But that photograph never existed, nor did the fatal moment I had expected when my brother squeezed the trigger. The phantom photographer would have had to destroy his plate, speechless before Sergeant Pyotr Goliadkin's corpse, cursing this bewildering flaw in the iron logic of honour. Pyotr's shot had lodged in my right arm with an explosion of smoke, flesh and blood, knocking me into the snow, shocked rather than wounded. The woods filled with flapping wings, vanishing into the sky, as the seconds rushed to my side, expecting the duel to have ended in the best way possible. Unforgiving of my brother's mistake, I summoned the strength to tell them to stand aside. Their flawed code of honour allowed me to shoot with my left hand, and Pyotr alone knew the damage it could inflict.

Last night, hesitating opposite the stairs leading to Thadeus Dreyer's bedroom, I reconstructed each moment as, lying on the ground, I shot the soldier who for me incarnated the most loathsome romanticism. I understood that that hand, which would this night soon kill another man with absurd allegiances to poetry, contained at that instant all my power and all my differences with the world. That I killed Pyotr with my left hand and was now about to visit the same proud slaughter on General Dreyer's old body

94

would tie together all the loose ends of a life dedicated to annihilating everything preposterously heroic in the human spirit. Nobody, I thought, could blame me for wanting to unite those two opposite lives and replace once and for all the mirage of the sacred with chaos, that unpardonable evil I smelled floating in the air once the echo of my shot had slowly disappeared among the hills and left my brother's corpse shrouded in the silent respect only death can bring.

By December 1917, only a few months after the duel, it was easy to join the Austrian infantry relief as a staff sergeant. The battered troops of the Austro-Hungarian Empire had already become a kind of sewer where those in flight from Russia, whether Cossacks or not, were welcomed like temporary heroes prepared to end their days in the trenches. It's true that my somewhat bilious appearance, Russian passport and threadbare German were constant sources of suspicion among my superiors, but in those days nobody could determine to which flag a man born on the banks of the Don swore loyalty. A few years earlier a hundred thousand Cossacks had been slaughtered in the Carpathians fighting the Prussians, and now an equal number battled on behalf of the Kaiser and the Emperor, hoping to snatch from Kerensky a patch of Russian land where they could bury their dead. The eternal, futile wanderings of Ukrainian horsemen, divided between loyalty to their race and the dubious promises of a nation they would one day receive as payment for their services, were played out again with the usual balance sheet of betrayals, massacres and disillusion. In the Ukraine, devastated by the Bolshevik revolution, White and Red Guards now mercilessly cut each other to pieces yet again, both sides using our mercenaries as cannon fodder. But many, like my brother, still denied the fact that a Cossack's fate can only be that of an exile or a survivor. Which is to say that doubting the loyalty of a Cossack in the First World War was an irrelevance, like wondering whether the Croats or Uhlans fighting on the Austrian side would remain loyal to the empire which had begun to dissolve into history as fast as a demon before evening Mass.

Needless to say, a war like that, an absolute catastrophe for everything my father and brother once believed in, was for me more than simply a refuge. It was a kind of inverted paradise, confirming my scepticism as if the war had been forged solely to justify my killing Pyotr and everything he represented. The last reserves of loyalty and poetry had been bled from me long ago on Ukrainian snow. All I retained was my withered arm, a desiccated stump which was enough to remind me of the reasons behind the duel and my radical denial of everything to do with what my father once called 'the divine order of things'. Nevertheless, on occasion that useless appendage – like the fin of a blind, repulsive fish – made me fear that my brother's death had not settled my business with his abhorrent idealism. That killing Pyotr had not succeeded in completely exterminating him or erasing the hated figure of my father tormented me. In some way it had conferred eternity upon them both. My brother had died without giving me time to show him the error of his ways and had deprived me of the pleasure of seeing his disillusion. His absence made me fragile; at times I began to fear that a part of my soul, tarnished by remorse or even compassion towards men, still cherished virtue. I could do little to rid myself of those doubts, and, though I did sometimes manage to forget them, they haunted me in a vivid, recurrent dream: I was back in the Ukraine, riding with my brother on the northern bank of the Don. A ragged regiment of Cossacks watched us silently from the other side, envying the naive calm with which Pyotr and I moved over that uncertain territory, which they could not reach. Suddenly I heard behind me the voice of my grandmother, the only person I ever felt anything like affection for, also making fun of the Cossack nation and laughing at the memory of the burial of the poet Lermontov, the last and most troublesome of the Romantics. She spoke without resentment but exhausted by eighty years of suffering on the shores of the Caspian, and she portrayed the poet's funeral as the final jest of a spoiled brat lacking in imagination.

'That wretch let himself be killed like Pushkin,' she muttered with one of those vague smiles one sees only in dreams. 'He didn't even have the guts to invent a death of his own,' and she described Lermontov's duel with the minute detail of someone telling an old joke only she finds funny.

Then Pyotr, in a rage, raised his whip and lashed my horse as if it were to blame for my grandmother's mockery. His blows provoked in me a sudden, consuming sadness rather than fury, and I lifted my left hand to take away the whip, which suddenly turned into my right arm, fragile and bleeding like a young hare. Pyotr was already galloping over the waves to join up with his Cossack regiment, proclaiming his victory over the traitor.

That dream travelled with me for months along the paths opened up by the war through the eastern confines of Europe. I saw the trenches of Bohemia, Bulgaria and, finally, Serbia, a one-armed spirit whose gun weighed less than the feeling of having a debt outstanding on the field of honour. Fortunately, the devastation spreading around me gradually dispersed those visions until, finally, when my regiment was sent to the Balkans, I thought they had vanished. It did not occur to me for a single moment that my duel against the spectres of my brother and father had only just begun. Destiny held back its best card, a reverse of fortunes that would delay for over forty years the resolution of the game Thadeus Dreyer and I were about to begin in a miserable, ravaged village on the banks of the Danube.

Among the few papers I could salvage from the mansion last night after Thadeus Dreyer's death – almost all related to his senile obsession with chess and the long years he spent in Switzerland after 1943 – I found a dozen loose sheets on which the general had at some stage tried to describe our encounter at the Balkan front and the reasons that led him to appropriate someone else's name. The narrative is, it must be said, confused in the extreme, rife with contradictions and reminiscences. Its disorder no doubt reveals the state of his soul during the months he lived in the village of Karanschebesch, the last outpost of the Austro-Hungarian Empire as it faced the disaster on the Danube. He appeared to me again as on the day I found him in my office: disconsolate, unable to hide his troubled adolescent hands and wanting from me an assurance I refused to give.

Tall and thin as a cathedral spire, Richard Schley had the air of an ascetic forced out of prolonged seclusion. At first glance, his gestures conveyed a confidence beyond his years, but it was easy to see behind them the seed of what would soon undermine his convictions. He had just come to the Balkans as deacon to our chaplain, Father Ignatz Wagram, a fanatical priest who was soon killed by mortar fire. The seminarist had been forced to assume the duties of priesthood while we waited for the Curia to send a replacement. Previously, when the two men passed my improvised duty office in Karanschebesch, they reminded me of a severed family not yet resigned to their orphan and widowhood. At that time the boy let himself be led by the war. Submissive to the point of delusion, he was always at the priest's side, hankering after heroism in a way that reminded me of my brother's raw idealism and made me instantly loathe him. Never, in the years we spent together, would he speak to me about his relationship with the priest, but Wagram's demise was clearly in great part responsible for Schley's spiritual chaos. Overnight the priest's death must have deprived him of all resistance to the realities of the horror, casting him on wasteland where only stubble grew, and where grim and fearsome events showed him the undeniable fact that there was no place for heroism, much less for the faith that had brought him to this point. One afternoon I heard him comment with a contrived firmness of tone, 'Goliadkin, sometimes I wonder whether Father Wagram didn't deserve a place in hell.'

I have to admit that at first I was embarrassed by being forced to listen to the confessions of a stranger. I soon learned, however, to hear the sound of rats scurrying underneath his words, and became convinced this man was my opportunity to complete my destructive mission, left unfinished by Pyotr's death. Perhaps destiny had brought me the seminarist so that, aided and abetted by the war, I could clear his path to the disintegration of his soul and keep him by my side, not a corpse on the field of honour, but alive, vital and vibrant in his disillusion.

But the youth was not going to surrender easily to my desire to trample his soul and preserve him like an eternal relic of the world's pettiness. One night, without warning, he announced that Father Wagram's relief had arrived, leaving him free to cross the Danube and save from the trenches an old friend of his called Thadeus Dreyer. Like a lover who won't accept being jilted, I tried to dissuade him from his suicidal journey. In vain I struggled to convince myself that a death in the trenches could be the only logical conclusion to a story like his. Circumstances now seemed set to repeat my brother's fate and leave me yet again with the memory of heroic, unbearded death. That youthful face reflected the spirit of someone who has lovingly bred a flock of pigeons and refuses to recognize they have become an intolerable plague. An echo resounding infinitely in his mind prevented the minimal acknowledgement of evil I needed to forget my brother's face forever. When this stubbornness forced him to go behind enemy lines to find the regiment of a man called Dreyer, all I could do was let him go and hope he would die of disillusionment before he found his lost unit and the faith Dreyer seemed to keep for him from some remote corner of his past. There was not much more I could do to aid his disintegration and etch on his features the eternal death agony I'd have preferred for Pyotr.

Sometimes, my grandmother used to say, it takes more than a beard or a scar to distinguish a man from his twin. The distinctions with which nature itself tries to make amends for the error of repetition are something else. They are usually subtle differences like a mole in a private place, a slight variation in the colouring of the eyes, or the preference for one hand that others would choose to see as an attribute of the devil. I still clearly recollect the afternoon in my childhood when my grandfather loaded the shopkeeper's mule with a gallon of vodka, a rope and an oak-handled whip with which he hoped to exorcise my left-handedness. The insults my grandmother flung then at her husband, her son-in-law and all those who believed until their dying day that exact symmetry was the only honourable, Christian way of negotiating life had no effect. My own mother had succumbed years before to the anger of that arrogant ataman who blindly trusted the strength of his arm and alcohol to right any fault, any disturbance, in the divine order of things. I do not know how far my grandfather thought he had corrected my sinister inclinations with a beating, but I'm sure that deep down, in some shadowy recess of consciousness, he realized nature would always, in the end, differentiate between his grandchildren. Over time, I have also reached the conclusion that his fears, his anger towards me and distinct favouring of my brother, were justified to a point. For my left-handedness did seem like a present from Lucifer, one of those slight privileges of transgression by which a twin could override the irony of seeing his own ageing, his own inescapable humanity, macabrely reflected in another face, artfully embodying what is most loathsome in himself.

Shortly before my regiment was transferred to Karanschebesch I returned home to attend my grandmother's funeral, and I discovered in the basement of my father's house the whip that had served to bleed my left-handedness out of me. Someone then told me my father had carried that nefarious weapon with him till the day when Turkish guns annihilated him in one of many wars the Cossacks fought for Mother Russia. I felt the same repulsion at the thought of that grotesque hero clinging to such an object as a symbol of his faith as I did over Pyotr's insignia or months later watching my young seminarist cross the Danube. That a Cossack should die for the Russians, begging for the mirage of an impossible, illusory fatherland – or that anyone should think it legitimate to risk his life for a fellow human being – seemed to me as absurd as the desire to bludgeon left-handedness out of a child. The rules governing this world are not, cannot be, of that nature. All we have left to us now is to beat a path leading irrevocably to the destruction of the sacred, and to accustom ourselves to the idea that poetry has no place in the melancholy corner of the universe in which we have been imprisoned. I have devoted every moment of my life since Pyotr's death to demonstrating that rituals of honour and loyalty are a privilege of the weak, and I want to believe that Dreyer at least came to understand that, in the three days he spent in the Balkan trenches searching for a recruit whose life was in the end less important than his name.

In the days following the seminarist's departure I wandered the camp trying to gather all the money and information that would help me survive in the coming chaos. I thus managed to find out about many of Dreyer's activities in the camp – almost all of them beyond the fringes of military regulations – which must have brought him substantial amounts of money as well as an enviable influence over his superiors. Those who met him and lived to tell the tale spoke of him with admiration and resentment, and quite a number confirmed my suspicion that he was not who he said he was. Given his undeniably Jewish features and strong Viennese accent, Thadeus Dreyer was clearly a pseudonym; my young seminarist had already told me as much. Nevertheless, rumour was rife in the camp that the recruit's conscience bore the marks of not one but countless substitutions, the nature of which nobody could explain. It was common in those times to steal someone else's identity, and I admit I always thought such impersonations confirmed unambiguously that men were capable of doing anything to survive at the front. However, the recruit who obsessed my young seminarist, and whom he had once called Jacob Efrussi, did not conform to my idea of impersonation as an invaluable means of survival. However much I tried, I couldn't understand why a Jew should have renounced his name not once but several times only to end up at the front. Jews were never highly regarded in the Austro-Hungarian Empire, and the great majority managed to benefit from a combination of this condition, their good fortune and the suspicion they provoked in gentiles to avoid being conscripted. Sometimes, therefore, I wondered if Dreyer was not driven by the same engine as me, and had found in war and deception a powerful means of survival. Had not the biblical Jacob also been the champion of impostors? Even so, with Dreyer the image of that kind of mystical fraudulence crumbled before the undeniable fact that he'd used his power not to trick others but to rid himself of the safety of numbers and the many names he'd stolen throughout his life.

It took the youth three days to return to Karanschebesch, and on each day Pyotr returned to torment my dreams. This time the dream had an additional, deeply disturbing dimension. Pyotr was no longer whipping my horse and I wasn't in the saddle; Thadeus Dreyer and the seminarist took turns in those roles in my nightmare as if in a mediocre farce. The Cossacks on the other side of the Don had disappeared and their place was filled by a faceless, nameless crowd whose uniforms seemed drawn from some grotesque, imaginary kingdom.

One evening I was awoken from that dream by the noise of hoofs on the cobbles of Karanschebesch. Someone outside shouted that the enemy had started to cross the Danube. The voice of alarm resounded off my office walls and finally forced its way into my head. I'd got to my feet and begun to look for the money and documents I'd prepared for my flight, when a two-headed shadow invaded my office, suddenly thrust from someone else's nightmare deep into mine. I made to lift my hand to my holster, but made out my young seminarist lurking under that mess of blood and mud, his face now sure and confident. It was as if his sojourn behind enemy lines had taken him past maturity to the brink of old age. Silently he had entered the disaster zone of my office with a body slung over his shoulder, which he now deposited lovingly on the ground with the sigh of someone throwing off a very heavy, useless piece of armour. I thought then that he had at last indelibly inscribed somewhere on his soul the mark of a survivor. This man, I thought, has lost his spirit, and I shall ensure he never gets it back. Meanwhile the seminarist loomed above me in splendid disarray. 'My name is Thadeus Dreyer,' he announced, suddenly emptying onto my desk a clinking savings box and a bundle of bloody passports, in which act I thought I at last recognized his submission to the laws of opprobrium, to my laws.

I remember I wanted to embrace him to welcome him to the world, but for a few seconds he stood to attention before his companion's body, as if waiting for his soul to depart the room for ever so he might take full possession of his name. Outside, the hoofs of the enemy cavalry were already ringing on the bridge over the Danube, thickening the crackling atmosphere of death and flight that already oppressed the roofs of Karanschebesch. For a moment, confused by the new Thadeus Dreyer's melancholy gesture, I wondered whether his strident imposture stemmed from motives other than those I had chosen to attribute to him.

In any case, the transformation the youth had undergone would bind us indissolubly. After all, the identity he'd appropriated came from other men, it no longer belonged to anyone but wandered the dark night of time, a ghostly mass which I would undertake to mould, though it might cost me my life.

Vienna welcomed us in December 1918 with the spectacle of its defeat. In our absence an entire universe, rather than just a war, seemed to have come to an end. At the front we'd become used to thinking each day would be our last, and our return home felt like the delirium of a dying soldier. Each face, each object, was part of the sad, muffled engine our conquerors had presented us with to drive the immense scrap-heap of empire. Schönbrunn's columns supported a pompous palace whose corridors were now presided over by empty fur coats and uniforms, rusty breastplates and standards which served only to wipe the dust from the ravaged shelves. A phantom crowd walked slowly past its walls, looked bitterly at the deserted parks, the closed cafés or the reflections of their own faces in the windows of shops displaying naked dummies and selling hats nobody would wear again. Time in the city had slowed down so brutally that on occasion it seemed non-existent.

For several weeks we roamed those avenues on a cart which Dreyer, at my insistence, had confiscated from a family of Poles unfortunate enough to cross our path. He did so reluctantly, threatening the itinerants regretfully as if putting down a sick dog he had had since childhood. Now, however, he seemed resolved to assume fully the consequences of his impersonation and deception. As soon as we returned to Austria he surrendered to my designs, submissive as a man whose sole aim was survival and who revered only naked power, stripped of the flimsy separation of good from evil. Prickly though obliging, he let me lead us through the dingy but happy disarray of prostitutes, drunken soldiers, merchants of death and multitudes hungry not for peace but for those grim desires which would lead us back to war a few years later. Even I was surprised by Dreyer's talent at such times for varying his masks of deceit. It was as if he'd decided to play out the full range of his collapse, every erring way, and was so successful that he almost managed to divest himself of the ingenuous spirit which had preceded the theft of Thadeus Dreyer's name. Gradually, during the years of bloodletting, revolution and upheaval that shook Austria after the First World War, Dreyer removed any obstacle that might put our survival at risk. When the memory of the youth he had been finally evaporated the only remaining task was the dirty business of prevailing, whatever the cost. A desire to transgress had developed at the centre of his being; nothing seemed powerful enough to contain it.

Soon my testimony about Thadeus Dreyer's actions at the Balkan front, helped by the odd coin distributed wisely in a country avid for heroes and worn down by successive revolutions, consecrated him as a war hero. A false record of daring exploits in the war, of which the failed rescue of his childhood friend was undoubtedly the most eloquent chapter, soon brought him the Iron Cross. He became one of many veterans plying the streets of Vienna or Berlin, parading the air of macabre respectability which, around 1932, was required by the rising National Socialist Party of Austria in order to impose itself on the remains of the German race. Dreyer cleverly displayed an exceptional thespian talent, appearing to the world a man of the strongest conviction, able to persuade multitudes to immolate themselves on behalf of the ideals of the party and the person of Hitler.

For the young Austrians and Germans who passed through his house, drawn by his decadent, magnificent orgies, his fiery articles in *Der Stürmer* or his promises of a great, collective future at the Führer's side, he was an incarnation of the pan-Germanic spirit. Party officers were quick to appreciate his skill at moulding those most reluctant to disappear into the smooth succession of marches and flags with which they hoped to paper over what were just the remnants of Austria and Germany. And so, a few days after Hitler established himself as Chancellor of the Third Reich, Dreyer was able to suggest to Hermann Goering a project that would become the symbol of his existence.

Dreyer spared me the details of his plan, but his objective was soon clear. In a word, what he'd proposed was that Goering should support him in the training of a small legion of impostors who would occasionally replace senior party officials in public appearances considered high-risk. The project was itself fairly risky, of course, and it's very likely that Goering himself, who accepted it enthusiastically, insisting on maximum discretion, was already toying with the possibility of making much more lucrative use of the impersonators than simply the protection of his colleagues and superiors. Whatever the truth of that may be, Dreyer pursued his ideas without stopping to ponder how ironic or compromising his situation was. He began to search the empire for grey hollow men, mature down-at-heel soldiers, impressionable adolescents and, above all, anxious chess players whom, later on, he would undertake to transform into pawns of real power. He moulded their physical appearance into living effigies of Nazi Party members, and scrubbed clean their lives and minds in order to inscribe there whatever he or his superiors thought useful. In fact, I doubt Dreyer ever believed his own reasons for dedicating his efforts to the creation of a host of impostors, since he cared very little then what the Nazis did or did not do. He was simply looking for the means to allow himself future access to the powerful, whatever their ideology. His life had finally fallen into a whirlpool from which not even he had any hopes of escaping. His single, real mission was to let himself be dragged along by the reckless course of his own existence. His preoccupations and destiny lay elsewhere. And only time, represented by the figure of an obscure young SS officer by the name of Adolf Eichmann, was to help him find once and for ever the means to shake off the savage hold of destiny.

Since his arrest a few weeks ago in Buenos Aires, Adolf Eichmann's name has been mentioned everywhere with loathing and contempt. Before the war, however, nobody could have foreseen that that name, its story and the crimes now attributed to it would come to symbolize those years. His colleagues always called him 'the Rabbi', and when you saw him it wasn't difficult to grasp where this nickname originated. Even among the hierarchy of the Nazi army, there was a degree of racial scepticism towards officers whose looks did not match the rigours of Aryan phrenology. In any case, Eichmann never admitted to knowing about the slanderous epithet. He'd been born in Solingen eight years before the start of the First World War and it was evident that his nondescript appearance, seasoned somewhat by facial features that looked suspiciously Semitic, must have caused the odd setback in the early days of his military career. That was perhaps why he nurtured such an angry hatred of Jews and dedicated himself to researching them exhaustively. As an adolescent he had learned to speak Hebrew with alarming fluency, and he could recite in full the innumerable Sabbath prayers. On the other hand, he rarely said anything about himself or the way he had managed to win General Heydrich's trust at an age and time when the majority of young Germans were hardly considering enlisting in the forces of the Reich. It was as if, to him, everything related to his previous life and his discreet, steep climb up the ladder of power was unimportant compared to the future he intended to forge for himself in the Nazi army. He always swayed markedly when he walked, like a little runaway locomotive tiring and tiresome as a result of an impossible impetus he managed to forget only when facing a chessboard. Only then did his body acquire the sphinx-like stillness which made his opponents lose their composure. I often counted the minutes it took him to move his pieces in particularly difficult games, and never, but never, did I see him blink twice in between moves.

We had met him in Prague in 1926, wandering through the last vestiges of the empire during the uncertain years of the Weimar republic. On Saturdays, Dreyer and I went to a rather disreputable-looking café which had the dubious honour of hosting the only chess circle in Bohemia. Every week about twenty individuals, who looked disturbingly alike, played there with religious devotion. Travellers, bureaucrats, weights-and-measures inspectors, legal clerks, all anxiously awaiting the end of the week in order to preside over those black-and-white worlds with Napoleonic greed. Dreyer overcame them all in a few sessions, and perhaps would have been content with this simple amateur show of strength if Eichmann had not burst into the café one afternoon. Eichmann asked to be black, and Dreyer agreed without too much conviction, pliantly, in fact, as if recognizing rules which had been set out years ago. On that occasion, time suspended as if in a daguerrotype, the game ended in stalemate. It was in the early hours that Eichmann, courteously commanding, asked his adversary to come to his hotel and engage in a fresh contest. But to my surprise Dreyer rejected the invitation, pretending that we had to leave immediately for Berlin. When we left the café he sighed, feeling obliged to give an explanation he had not been asked for: 'Take my word for it, Goliadkin. That boy is sick, very sick.'

But it was he who collapsed that night from tertian fever which lasted at least a month, and he who was so ill that I started to think the encounter had torn out his love of chess and life by the roots.

We met young Adolf Eichmann several times after that, but Dreyer did all he could to postpone the game they had both left pending in that Prague café. Eichmann himself soon understood there are some things a man must avoid to preserve his sanity, and so accepted the alternative offer of a close camaraderie which, without becoming a real affection, brought them closer than I was comfortable with. It is true that, behind his apparent mediocrity, Eichmann revealed an enviable ability to manipulate and destroy his peers, which he always did in the conviction that their annihilation was necessary to help reorder the world. For men like him or my father, evil, death and violence do not exist for themselves, but as instruments of transition towards a mythical, morally correct order which nevertheless carries the unerring sign of the chaos to which we are condemned. Though it is true my own forays with Thadeus Dreyer also negotiated harsh necessities of destruction, I was never tempted to admire Eichmann's ravaging spirit. I would rather have believed in my brother's uncompromising goodness or the painful scruples of the not quite forgotten seminarist of Karanschebesch, than have submitted to Adolf Eichmann's utilitarian evil, which I considered even cruder and, consequently, less tolerable than the blindest act of philanthropy.

In recent weeks there has been much speculation over the extent to which Eichmann contributed to the great massacre of the Jews that took place during the Second World War. I am sure, however, that the obscure petrol salesman, promoted by Himmler to captain within a few years, at heart lacked the degree of courage necessary to grasp the real dimension of the evils he was engaged in unleashing.

One night, in the middle of 1942, Eichmann came to our small flat in Berlin to tell us that in Wannsee General Reinhard Heydrich had ordered him to take charge of the extermination of those Jews still left in the Reich. Up to that moment, the fate of the Jews had been obscure, consistently couched in political or legal euphemisms like *mobilization* or *deportation* which at least made it possible to deceive oneself. But Eichmann's words now left no room for any ambiguity. Such indiscretion would have been astounding from any officer of the Reich but especially so coming from a man like him.

We soon discovered that, perhaps overawed by the mission he was about to take on, Eichmann had sought out Dreyer to beg him – almost order him – to play the game they had postponed so often. As soon as we saw him come in, serious and distraught like a criminal on death row, we understood something bestial and definitive was about to snap free within that man, the shadow of a scruple which needed to be subdued by victory over Dreyer. That night, overwhelmed by Eichmann's confession, Dreyer offered little resistance. He lost or allowed himself to be beaten in three successive games, while Eichmann, unable to concentrate, pontificated against the Jews, stating every possible reason why the regime had decided to charge him with their extermination. Dreyer, for his part, let him talk sense-lessly till dawn, and at times allowed the impression that his was the complicitous, affirming silence his adversary had been seeking.

However, the following day Dreyer demanded I accompany him immediately to Vienna. The complaisance of the previous night had entirely disappeared from his face, replaced by the presence of mind of someone who has at last discovered the real purpose of his life. When we arrived in Vienna, a dreadful, icy drizzle was falling on the city. I suggested we should take refuge in a modest pension on the outskirts, but Dreyer insisted we went straight to the city ghetto. It was pouring when we finally arrived among the remnants of what had been the jewellery shop of one Isaac Efrussi. Here and there the water still washed away charred wood and sharp bits of glass. Nobody was there to tell us when or how the devastation had happened. There, on the steps to the shop, the infinite sadness swirling in Dreyer's thoughts emerged in a long, low lament for the memory of that old jeweller, who we'd never hear of again.

From that night on Dreyer's encounters with Colonel Eichmann multiplied alarmingly. United by their passion for chess, they were locked for hours in conversations which inevitably concluded with what Eichmann called the

Jewish problem. While they talked, Dreyer maintained the attitude of a pupil waiting to receive precise instructions on how to blow up a bridge or carry out an assassination. But when Eichmann left, my companion would collapse on the sofa, drink to excess and frequently embark on feverish, incoherent monologues. Such was his despondency that I began to fear for his life. Not that, in itself, his life was of great importance to me. Ever since our meeting in the Balkans I'd distanced myself from the slightest bond of affection that might curb my plan to destroy Dreyer's soul. If I wanted to keep him alive, it was in order to enjoy his destruction, to prolong it as long as possible. I wanted particularly to prevent him from dying like my brother: a slave to heroism. That's why, after Eichmann's visit and our trip to Vienna, I was struck by the fear that the annihilation of a Thadeus Dreyer suddenly suffused by doubt, before he'd fully taken on the disillusionment I'd always wished on him, might be the work of other hands than mine. In a word, I was afraid that at any moment Dreyer, in turmoil after the recent reminder of Jacob Efrussi, would be stupid enough to murder Eichmann (or die in the attempt), convinced that would somehow settle his own accounts with life and mankind.

I began to understand then that the day we visited the Vienna ghetto had set Dreyer on a path of tortuous self-examination, during which his unhappiness, loyalties and passions would undergo a strange readjustment. The man I had begun to consider the exemplary victim of the world's miseries suddenly began to reclaim his soul. A weighty scruple, rekindled overnight, began to make him hesitate on the brink of arbitrariness or dishonour. Ethics for Dreyer were now a slippery substance he strove to keep under control at any cost. He suddenly started to invent contorted moral justifications for each of his acts, however vile they might appear, and negotiated life brandishing an impossible code of values which really only made more painful the conviction that had once taken him to the Balkan front, that reality would always triumph over the promises of redemption. Certainly, my fellow traveller had acquired his new name with enviable ease, as if emerging from a chrysalis, but now even he couldn't believe the motives he had proffered. Just like the one-time empire that collapsed before our eyes, then to be sucked implacably back into war, something within him resisted recognizing that his new name was written in the grim roll-call of the disenchanted. Despite my initial conviction, I soon had to accept that an idea of the sacred hadn't been completely driven from his soul that afternoon in Karanschebesch, but had merely been in abeyance – though still strong enough to bore into his degenerate conscience like a small chisel. My relationship with him then felt like a long, precarious marriage, with each partner locked into his own soliloquy, searching for some light in the murky labyrinth where Eichmann had cast us like a pair of Cretan princesses.

I suppose that was when Dreyer began to entertain the strange idea that his identity as an impostor obliged him to repay the world's sins against all the men – against all the dead – he had inherited with the name of Thadeus Dreyer, or, maybe, just those against the one man whose life he'd assumed in the 1914 war: the Jew Efrussi.

Initially it must have been only that – an idea, the remnant of a scruple – translated into a spirit of redemption which, naturally, I found disconcerting. After his last encounter with Eichmann our time was spent in a constant struggle in which my efforts to cast him back down into the abyss of infamy confronted his relentless remorse. It was as if destiny had sentenced me for eternity to put a bullet through my brother's insignia, only to see him resurrected again and again, a thousand times. Now that everything has turned out for the worst, now that it's of no consequence what may happen to me or what happened last night to Dreyer, I recognize that, in those grievous days, I was afraid more than once that my companion was in effect a kind of holy man destined to restore order to a landscape I needed to be as fragmentary and wretched as our souls. Dissatisfied and unable until then even to guide his own steps, from that night Dreyer gave himself over to the task of righting others' destinies. His commitment was so radical that I thought he would be overcome by what he now believed to be his unanswerable obligation to the Jews, a race whose history of exile and chimerical promises, perhaps too close to that of the Cossacks, always led me to consider it one of the most contemptible parts of creation.

The first, almost imperceptible, signs of my defeat started to emerge. Instead of fulfilling his commitments to the Reich's war effort, Dreyer stayed in bed and pleaded sickness, absorbed in deep but no doubt eventful thought. His manoeuvres in Berlin, his meetings with Goering, and the Führer's increasingly incendiary speeches – not to mention the war hero's facile glory that we'd created from the stuff of his Balkan exploits – no longer attracted him. He didn't dare detach himself entirely from the illusion we'd forged together, but now took every opportunity to warn me that the war was lost, that it had been a mistake to believe in the Nazis.

Things were heading in that direction when Dreyer took the decision he'd silently been contemplating since the night he played his final game against Eichmann. One morning he awoke from a bout of interminable lethargy and shouted, 'Kretzschmar is our man, Goliadkin.'

It took me a few seconds to comprehend the true weight of his words, but very soon I understood what they implied and it terrified me. I knew Dreyer had for some weeks been contemplating the substitution of Eichmann, but until that moment refused to admit he'd always known the right person for the job. Ever since Dreyer had spoken to Marshal Goering, his small band of doubles had performed marvellously: more than once the good offices of one or another had saved men like Himmler or Goebbels. Some high-ranking officers were beginning to have reservations about the efficient use of impostors whose loyalty was, after all, to Goering, but none of them ever contemplated the possibility of the complete substitution Dreyer now intended to accomplish, not within the Reich's High Command but with the less prominent if perhaps more dangerous person of Colonel Eichmann. There's now little point in wondering whether Dreyer once thought this sub-stitution might be the first of many, for I think the only enemy to defeat, as far as he was concerned, was the man directly responsible for the Nazi extermination campaign. Consequently, when he declared Kretzschmar was the double he needed, I felt as if someone had turned an hour-glass over before me and time would run out too soon.

I did not have to ask him what had led to this decision. Young Kretzschmar, with whom he enjoyed much closer ties than those binding an officer to a subordinate, was undoubtedly the best of his men, the one who owed him most loyalty, and the only one who seemed prepared to do absolutely anything for him. Dreyer had always shown a disproportionate degree of affection towards Kretzschmar. More than once, intrigued by the secret attention and money he gave him over several years, I came to the conclusion that this mutual affection was not just the result of what the general called an ancient debt of friendship owed to the wretched youth's father.

Whatever the case, there was no doubt Kretzschmar was the ideal person for his plans. Apart from being more or less Eichmann's age, he was one of the top chess players in Berlin. Physically, his complexion matched perfectly the SS officer's, and it was easy to imagine that his features would offer no resistance to the expertise of the magnificent surgeons Marshal Goering had put at our disposal. Ravaged by the endless orgies held by the Nazi Youth, the young man had that wraith-like quality of people who, while living only for uncertainty, revenge and hatred, have created an aura of indifference which renders them virtually imperceptible. I must confess that in the years when I followed his every move on Dreyer's express instructions, these blurred edges often brought to mind the decadent ambiguity of the Adolf Eichmann we had met in Prague. An ill-concealed baldness had begun to show round Kretzschmar's military cap with evident designs on his appearance, which it seemed to want to destroy completely. His nose and eyes were minimal features on the topography of his face, and the rest of his body, slightly stooping as if always facing a chessboard, suggested the malleability of an empty suit which only the capricious to and fro of the wind could inject with an impression of vitality. Nobody would think him capable of perpetrating a crime, but he behaved towards Dreyer with the abject submission of a bastard vassal. He chatted, studied, obeyed orders and played chess, never losing sight of the objective of his efforts. In short, everything about the youth vindicated Dreyer's choice, so much so that I'd have bet my healthy arm on him if only I could have recruited him to my side. Dreyer had cultivated and won his loyalty by defeating him at chess; his soul belonged to Dreyer as if it were his creation. Hence, when asked if he really thought his protégé would have the presence of mind necessary to replace Eichmann on Dreyer's terms, the general nodded irritably, as if the question were too obvious or too personal to be posed by someone who, like me, knew little of the ins and outs of chess and the immutable code of honour it enforced on its loyal subjects.

My close relationship with Dreyer was re-established in the weeks after he saw the light. As his plans to substitute Adolf Eichmann became as viable as they were compelling, his trust in my good offices was restored and he sketched for me the fine detail of how Kretzschmar was to be placed in command of the SS Department of Jewish Investigations. Everything was fitting into place without mishap, just as Dreyer had planned. The youth showed himself ready from the start to obey and submit to the rigorous system the general used to erase the minds of his disciples and prepare them to take on new identities. After the miraculous work of Goering's surgeons, Kretzschmar was soon physically suitable to replace Eichmann, and Dreyer thought the occasion might arise at any moment.

As the war progressed, Eichmann's influence over the Reich's policies increased dramatically, and, although the extermination of the Jews was still kept secret, there were serious rumours that his trains of death were daily packed with thousands of whom nothing more was ever heard. Colonel Eichmann's discipline, his profound knowledge of overland transport and his hatred of the Jews had turned him into a perfect engine of destruction, making it increasingly difficult to imagine that his obsession with chess could ever be strong enough for him to stake on one game the power he must have coveted since adolescence. Dreyer never doubted, however, that Eichmann would be prepared to give him a rematch – and stake his life on the result – when he introduced his champion to him. On the other hand, he never contemplated the possibility that Kretzschmar might be defeated by the SS officer. If the contest did eventually take place, it would be because he had first demonstrated his own superiority over the young man, and was as sure of Kretzschmar's ability to defeat Eichmann as he was of his own skills in the game. Kretzschmar represented the kind of impenetrable armour Dreyer had lacked when playing the colonel. It remained only to convince Eichmann to wager his identity against Kretzschmar for Dreyer's plans to begin to take on the shape he wanted. And if Eichmann, at a given moment, won or refused to accept defeat, Dreyer would kill him then and there.

But Thadeus Dreyer and his young chess champion had set out their plans with a chess player's impeccable logic, an unreal logic which depended largely on a concept of honour not to be expected of certain men. Not for one moment did they imagine they might be betrayed before Dreyer even had the opportunity to propose this final game to Eichmann. All it took was for me to send an anonymous letter to Himmler for him to order our immediate arrest and orchestrate the brutal destruction of the team of doubles Dreyer had been preparing under General Goering's auspices. Accused of collaborating with a Semitic conspiracy uncovered a few weeks earlier, Dreyer's adoptive sons disappeared one by one from their homes and barracks. As to young Kretzschmar, we didn't have time to find out his fate, but it would not be rash to suspect he ended his days in the Gestapo's cells. Conscious of how important it was for me to keep Dreyer alive, before sending the letter to Himmler, I'd established a providential link with the British secret service and the Swiss authorities in order to facilitate our escape. I almost had to kidnap Dreyer when the persecution began. Determined to find out what happened to Kretzschmar and the other impostors, he did all he could to stay in Berlin; however, when he realized it was too late to do anything to help them, he resigned himself to the necessity of escape, an act of cowardice which would undoubtedly poison the rest of his days.

From then on I was totally convinced that the natural order of things was on the side of men like myself. My hope that one day I would be favoured with the delightful contemplation of a man's total devastation was realized with chilling immediacy. It would have been a true miracle for Dreyer to have recovered from the blow I dealt his final attempt to save himself. Now hidden behind the name of Woyzec Blok-Cissewsky, a dead Polish baron, Dreyer sought refuge in Geneva like a wounded animal. And when he felt that snow, distance or anonymity wasn't enough to allow him to forget his failure, he sought in the labyrinths of chess that single obscure realm where an opponent would comply with rules no longer operative in the real world. For him, war and existence had ended alongside his plans to save the Jews, and I suppose that's why he hardly flinched when, in 1945, he learned the Russians had entered Berlin and that the name Eichmann didn't figure among those accused at Nuremberg. Divine justice had already had a chance to halt the infamy, and had allowed it to happen as if Eichmann were part of the sacred balance of forces underpinning the history of mankind. It mattered little that a man responsible for so many deaths had escaped justice. For Dreyer, this was and had to be an unbreakable law of reality, which he could do nothing to change.

I always thought Thadeus Dreyer's final destruction would be so pleasing to contemplate that I'd be able to live with it for years on end. Time, however, revealed that even that kind of pleasure can become tedious. Like a man who eventually develops contempt for the woman he desired and pursued for years, the remnant Thadeus Dreyer had become after our escape began to bore me. Senile, self-absorbed, obsessed by the games of chess he played by correspondence or those published daily in the little fascicles he collected with morbid care, the old man managed to bring me to the point where contempt can turn into compassion. Alarmed by the disloyalty I was verging on perpetrating against myself, the only thing I'd never allow,

I began to distance myself from him like someone foreswearing a pleasure which may be the death of him. I abandoned him in Geneva, resolved never to see him again.

But that ghost, like my brother's, would not let me go so easily. Two weeks ago, almost at the same time as Adolf Eichmann's arrest was announced in Argentina, Dreyer phoned me at an ungodly hour and asked me to come and see him immediately: 'You're my only friend, Goliadkin,' he explained. 'I have something very important to tell you about Eichmann.'

Instead of the triumphant tone I'd have expected as a result of Eichmann's arrest, his voice sounded extremely pained. Some time ago, when Dreyer sank into his manic passion for chess, I'd come to think the general was searching, half-heartedly, for Eichmann in the countless games he began to unravel in newspapers and publications from the most esoteric chess clubs. But I never thought he'd have any success with these bizarre methods. Had he found him at last? Was it him, in fact, who'd finally denounced Eichmann to Israeli justice? The brittle tone of his voice suggested otherwise; his call revealed the confusion of someone who has discovered something shocking – or gone out of his mind. Indeed, I thought later on, it mattered little to me whether the old man had something to tell me about Adolf Eichmann or not. What most worried me was his presumption of my loyalty and, worse still, the slight but betraying tremor of joy I'd felt on hearing him appeal to our friendship. Dreyer, I told myself (making an effort, like someone chasing off an evil thought), could take his guilt to hell with him, together with his friendship and his senile poetry. But he'd do so when I decided, before the Jews granted him the consolation of executing Eichmann. As I hung up I realized the time had come to kill him, having first revealed my treachery. If Dreyer thought I was the only friend he had, this was the time to strip him of this last poetic sentiment and frighten off the strange spectre of goodness which had somehow appeared from a recess of my consciousness.

Enthusiasm and dismay together spread through me last night as I headed towards Dreyer's house. It seemed my brother's shade was at last about to depart from my life, my guilt and my nightmares. Snow, or dusk or garden walls could easily bring back memories of him and the early morning in the Ukraine when I killed him. My hell, I thought as I climbed the stairs, still trying to shake off the tart memory of gunpowder, would soon end along with my life's mission. After all, with so many years spent struggling to destroy Dreyer, didn't I also deserve a little justice? I was soon to see, however, that even this happiness would be denied me. My eyes were still adjusting to the semi-darkness on the landing when I heard the front door slam, the house echoing like a church, as though someone had been hiding on the ground floor and waited for me to go upstairs to make their escape. When I entered his room, I saw Dreyer's body slumped over the chessboard, all his truth and sadness bleeding from a bullet wound someone else had left in the back of his neck. A shock of white hair covered his eyes and his right hand was stretched out across the board in front of him as if wanting to stop forever the echo of the shot that left him shrouded in the silent respect only death can bring.

IV

FROM NAME TO SHADOW

Daniel Sanderson

London, 1989

I suppose there are many ways to end a story, but the murder of Baron Blok-Cissewsky isn't one of them. Nor is it really the beginning of what I want to relate. It's something else – a violent detour in the huge domino effect in which he was doubtless a key piece, but not the only, and certainly not the first to fall. His story, like that of any remarkable individual, entails others less baroque. Mine, for example. I wouldn't try to put myself on the baron's level; I simply believe that one's own memory is the only certainty most of us can appeal to when reconstructing the past. That's why I've decided to tell this the way it happened to me and those like me, who had the dubious honour of being counted among the old man's heirs. I hope my lack of narrative skill won't offend all those ghosts who would surely have preferred to hear it in another order and from other lips.

Since what I'm about to tell is closely bound to the baron's posthumous whimsy, I've no choice but to begin by relating the strange details of his last will and testament, found inside a bottle of port the day after the crime. In that unmistakable handwriting of a Carmelite nun, Mr Woyzec Blok-Cissewsky (officer of the Polish army, retired) left a savings box of old coins to his aide Alikoshka Goliadkin, and directed that the rest of his few possessions in Switzerland should be sold, with the proceeds going to a sanatorium in Frankfurt. Later, in a printed postscript, the old man made three additions to his will: to Maestro Remigio Cossini, Sicilian painter, to Mr Deman Fraester, Flemish actor, and to me, his third and most frequently thrashed chess opponent by correspondence, he left the far from negligible sum of one hundred thousand Swiss francs each, which we could receive only in person, at his funeral.

Years later the Swiss press, trying to rekindle interest in an event it had perhaps not fully savoured at the time, hinted at the existence of an earlier will in which the baron had left his entire fortune to Mr Goliadkin, war invalid and the baron's companion in misfortune for at least forty years. True or not, I must insist that the first-will hypothesis, thought-provoking though it may be, in no way alters the substance of my tale. Whether or not Goliadkin, obsessed with that chimerical will, could have so brutally betrayed his friendship with Baron Blok-Cissewsky matters little. In some cases knowing who committed a crime is not enough to understand its motivation or discover all the faces hiding behind a bloody deed. I should point out that this will not really be the baron's story, or Alikoshka Goliadkin's, but the story of the obscure forces that led to their ruin and dragged us down with them.

A rail strike in London meant I missed Baron Blok-Cissewsky's funeral. I know no one expected a miracle in my race across half of Europe against the rapid decomposition of a corpse, but the Swiss city still welcomed me with the gloomy indifference reserved for those of us destined always to arrive late. The habitual resignation with which I prepared to face my ticking-off from Blok-Cissewsky's executors dissipated momentarily, however, thanks to the unexpected appearance of Maestro Remigio Cossini, who was waiting for me in Geneva central station with the forlorn patience of a distant relative.

Maestro Cossini was a shortish man who at first sight looked like a retired samurai. For a moment, seeing him emerge from a multitude of American executives and surly travellers, I thought he was a Japanese tourist who had been directed here because it was the city's most photogenic spot. But one had only to look him in the eye to know he was no ordinary man. As this occurred to me, I found his hand shaking mine firmly and his friendly, authoritative voice stating our names like a man not inclined to waste time on unnecessary explanations. Before I could respond, he led me out of the station and hailed a taxi which took us to the hotel, where Fraester waited to accompany us to the executor's office.

During the drive, the painter spoke with respectful familiarity, peppering his English with Italian expressions so blunt that they clashed with his refined manner. After reassuring me about the effect my lateness would have on the will, he devoted all his energies to informing me that the investigations into Baron Blok-Cissewsky's murder had taken an unexpected and apparently decisive turn. The day after the Baron's funeral, said the painter, the police had found Mr Alikoshka Goliadkin, Blok-Cissewsky's former assistant, dying in a cheap hotel in Cruseilles from a gunshot wound he'd inflicted to his own right temple. This, of course, allowed the local authorities to close this shameful case for good, to the great approval of that city's long-suffering residents.

'Obviously,' he concluded with an ease which struck me at the time as inscrutable, 'I'm telling you this so you understand from the start that this business contains more shit than we suspected.'

He spoke as if we'd known each other for years and had spent the last few weeks together in detailed analysis of the circumstances of the baron's death. Only later would I come to understand Cossini's rather unusual and petulant assertiveness; for him, the most intricate stories always appeared awesomely clear, while conversely, blatantly obvious official truths were those most worthy of suspicion. The alternative, febrile universe of his brain wouldn't allow Cossini to sit and wait for the rest of us mortals to catch up with his deductions, and his bald declarations were often insufferable, his words tinged with an intellectual haughtiness that might have been a naivety bordering on rank stupidity and which assumed that everyone could see what he saw and understand absolutely anything, no matter how intricate. I came to realize this during the brief time I spent with him, beginning that morning in Geneva. And I must add that I'm immensely grateful to him for it.

Remigio Cossini's warning about the murky circumstances which had brought us to Switzerland began to bear out as soon as we reached the hotel. On the last leg of the journey, the painter had unilaterally moved the conversation on to our common ground of chess, announcing that Mr Fraester supported his hypothesis that towards the end of his days our hapless benefactor had either lost his reason or been trying to warn us that something was about to happen. At least this time I had no trouble understanding what the man was talking about: my last epistolary contests with Baron Blok-Cissewsky, who usually subjected his play to rigorous analysis, had veered off into the most disconcerting heterodoxy. Impassive before each of my attacks, the old man had suddenly taken it into his head to compose pyrotechnic finales and strategies with the sole aim of crowning all his pawns, while the rest of the action on the board seemed absolutely insignificant.

'Fraester claims it's a typical case of senile dementia,' muttered Cossini, smiling for the first time since we'd met. 'But I'm not so sure.'

How the painter related those chess aberrations to the baron's misfortune or our own place in it was something he didn't disclose. Perhaps because I was beginning to get used to his cryptic comments, I chose not to ask him what had prompted those reflections, just as, I'm sure, Fraester hadn't done either.

Unlike Remigio Cossini, the Flemish actor turned out to be typical of his race, though a somewhat decadent version of it – almost a caricature. Obstreperous and blustering to the point of making a scene, Fraester was the polar opposite of the painter's laconic elegance. When I saw him approaching the taxi, tall and solid as a sequoia, I noticed in his gait a nervous rocking of the torso which at first I put down to an over-familiarity with amphetamines. Later I came to realize that the human-pendulum effect was caused by a severe limp, his left leg having been injured in his job as a movie double. From his clothes and manners, it was clear the man had seen better days, and now all he could do was trust providence to pay off innumerable debts, from gambling, or some more sinister source. I thought it impossible to associate that anthropoid with the game of chess, or any activity requiring a minimum of common sense. It soon became clear to me, however, that Fraester belonged to that tiny band of subnormal beings who, at nature's whim, are authentic prodigies when faced with a chessboard. Cossini had come to the same conclusion after his first conversation with the actor and so, as I gathered during our brief ride to the executor's office, had resigned himself to communicating with Fraester solely on matters to do with chess, exchanges which always ended in the most uncomfortable silences.

'Excuse the question, my friend,' the painter whispered to me, exhausted, while the actor announced us to the executor's secretary, 'but I'd love to know what the hell the baron could have seen in this utter imbecile.'

The executor's secretary's answer spared me from having to improvise a reply. Evidently nervous, the man told us the baron's executor had had to leave the country at short notice, but in there, he added, in his boss's office, someone was waiting who could reliably attend to our requests.

'We haven't come to request anything,' exclaimed Fraester, jovially sarcastic, 'we've come to pick up our money.'

The executor's assistant apologized, assuring us he had nothing to do with this distressing business, then confined himself to leading us through a complex labyrinth of cubicles, filing cabinets and extremely suspicious-looking clerks.

A man of indeterminate age, remarkable only because of a grotesque resemblance to the actor Humphrey Bogart, received us in the executor's office with grudging politeness. He spoke English with an accent as neutral as his demeanour, performing real marvels in his attempt to keep his American cigarette, unlit during the entire meeting, straight between his lips. He introduced himself with an impossible to remember name and immediately insinuated he knew almost everything about us. Without warning he began to list one by one the most shameful secrets of our résumés with a miniaturist's delectation. He began by stating that it didn't require a genius to realize the name Remigio Cossini was clearly invented, although on the other hand, he added, a forger could call himself whatever he liked, since the true strength of that vocation depended on the most cowardly anonymity. He didn't bother to clarify whether Fraester was a stage name or not, but declared his disdain for movie doubles, especially if, as seemed the case with Mr Fraester, they'd lost even the physical capacity to imitate the most second-rate of actors. As for me, concluded our host, it was a shame my best books were available only in second-hand bookshops these days, under the names of supposedly illustrious ladies and gentlemen whose fame, in spite of everything, had not been able to outshine the stylistic infelicities of their ghost writer. In short, our executor's stand-in humiliated us outright and without cause that afternoon, emphasizing our combined condition as usurpers, an attack which, coming from a man who was meant to be representing someone else, was thus made even more offensive to its bewildered and furious targets.

When I recall that scene, I can't think what kept us from reacting with dignity to the fake Bogart's aspersions. Perhaps their truth was simply too blatant to merit an evasion. Or maybe our passivity came from a vague fear that a confrontation with that individual, so enigmatic and self-confident, might jeopardize the happy turn of fate that had brought us this far. So none of us dared reply, though our cowardice or caution later proved of little use in preventing Baron Blok-Cissewsky's easy inheritance slipping suddenly from our grasp. Bogart's offensive diatribe turned out to be just the preamble to an even more disquieting declaration than the details of our lives, along the lines that none of us deserved to reach out a hand and collect the baron's juicy fortune. Then, looking exhausted, Bogart closed the door and invited us to sit down.

'I'm sorry you've come such a long way,' he muttered, fanning his cigarette with the folder in his hand. 'For the good of humanity, individuals like yourselves should move around as little as possible. If you're wondering why I'm here, it's to tell you Baron Blok-Cissewsky's last will and testament is, in a word, as illegitimate as each of you.'

The man seemed frankly sick of the scene, as if repulsed by everything there. Apparently expecting something more than our astonished stares, he waited in silence before continuing. The issue, he said at last, was terribly simple: like us, the late Baron Blok-Cissewsky was an impostor, so skilled in his art, truth be told, that it was virtually impossible to discover his real name.

'We have,' he said in a plural more mysterious than majestic, 'a list of at least seven different names and identities this man usurped over his life span, including Schley, Dreyer and a few more, till he came to Blok-Cissewsky. So, I'm afraid, gentlemen, you'd have great difficulty proving the validity of a will signed with a pseudonym and whose beneficiaries are themselves beings of, shall we say, dubious authenticity.'

Having passed sentence, he was unmoved by the displeasure of the baron's beneficiaries. I believe it was Fraester who then summoned sufficient courage to display his disagreement openly.

A gesture from Bogart was enough to bring the actor back to order. 'I haven't finished yet, Mr Fraester,' he said with the confidence of a lion-tamer. 'Of the baron's various identities, we're interested in only one: Thadeus Dreyer, a colleague of Hermann Goering's from early in the Second World War.'

With those words, the man revealed the real nature of this interview. It seemed he and whoever had sent him considered the baron one of many war criminals who'd managed to evade Allied justice and end their days concealed in a false identity. But how were we implicated in the baron's past? Why disturb his grave, now that a murderous or righteous hand had anticipated Bogart and his underlings' investigations? The same questions must have been crossing Fraester's and Cossini's minds at the time, though the words Cossini addressed to our improvised inquisitor were once again, several steps ahead of my thoughts.

'I don't particularly care, my good sir, if in the past the baron was a murderer or a saint,' said the painter, leaning over the desk and into the would-be Bogart's face. 'Nor do I want to know if you're a Nazi-hunter. Just tell me what the hell you want with us.'

As if these words had also been written in his own script, Bogart received Cossini's question without batting an eyelid. The eternal cigarette remained triumphantly straight between his lips while his hands stayed hidden in the depths of his trenchcoat. 'I think you and I are going to reach an understanding, Maestro,' he predicted, holding the painter's gaze.

And he went on to say that it would be simple to bypass these legal obstacles to Mr Blok-Cissewsky's will, and even increase the amount of our inheritances, if we would be so kind as to hand over, as soon as possible, a certain manuscript the baron had sent us a few weeks before his death.

The three beneficiaries exchanged surprised glances as insincere as they were unconvincing. There was no point denying Blok-Cissewsky had indeed recently sent us a document, which I'd received together with his final moves, consisting of annotations for a chess manual in Polish. I couldn't be sure that Cossini and Fraester had been entrusted with similar manuscripts, but the circumstances we found ourselves in suggested so.

'But it's only a chess manual,' I hurried to declare before my companions were stupid enough to deny the obvious truth. Bogart, regarding me with something like compassion, replied, 'A cryptogram, my dear sir. We believe that the manual contains enough hard evidence to hang Colonel Adolf Eichmann, whom we arrested a few weeks ago in the city of Buenos Aires.'

He said this as if pleading for clemency from an invisible judge, with a gentleness so contrary to his initial attitude, that it led us to suspect his intentions still further. We had no reason to doubt him – in the circumstances the most natural thing would have been to exchange the bundles of yellowed pages for a sum of money large enough to change our lives radically and help convict a war criminal. Nevertheless, that initial humiliation, the painful reminder coming from an individual of such suspect authority, wrought a dramatic transformation in our scale of values, if only for a couple of hours. Suddenly that final gesture of faith, from a man who we still felt incapable of the slightest fault, must have given us a rare and dreadful sense of self-importance and intensified the mistrust Bogart had sown in our minds. The old man seemed to have chosen us carefully, precisely because of our endlessly petty, dependent condition, in the hope we'd be the kind capable of resisting this too obvious and suspect temptation, and thereby preserving a secret that had poisoned his entire life.

Bogart must also have noticed this blunder in his method, the consequence of a premature underestimation of his opponents. In an instant he changed strategies, and refrained from asking whether we agreed to his proposal; now he'd have to go after us another way, privately and better armed. The offer, he announced before we left the meeting, was still on the table. He would remain at our disposal at the prefecture if, as he hoped, we decided to heed our consciences as upright men and, in exchange for more than merely moral rewards, hand over what Israeli justice needed to make itself felt at last throughout our wounded planet.

Once Bogart had left us alone, Cossini went over to the office window and stood there for a few seconds, his hands on the executor's desk. Finally he smiled meaningfully and muttered, 'If that man is a defender of humanity, I'm Rembrandt reincarnated. Trusting to his good intentions would be as stupid as believing Goliadkin could have lodged a bullet in his own right temple with his missing right hand.'

He pronounced this from that obscure place where, as I've said, painstaking reflection combined his unique intuition about human nature with his profound knowledge of the world's most obscure byways. Neither Fraester nor I bothered to try to untangle the reasons behind this conclusion. His words had the unquestionable authority of someone who knew too well the reverses of fortune. In fact, accepting his Delphic utterance was not difficult, for at least it offered us the illusion of a safe port on this stormiest of nights.

A couple of hours later, the painter, supremely confident, telephoned me in the hotel to announce that according to his calculations Fraester would give in at any moment to the fake Bogart's offer. This time the painter's conviction struck me as frankly ridiculous, and I was compelled to ask what made him think the actor would so easily and quickly break what I, by then, considered a blood pact between us.

'Don't take it the wrong way,' answered Cossini, 'but I know how to recognize a poor wretch when I see one.' And he hung up as if he wanted to give me some time for the news to sink in.

Things happened just as he predicted. The next morning Cossini and I each received a business card, the back of which announced the actor's decision to surrender his manuscript, inviting us to follow his wise example. Although Cossini had predicted this, the news hit me as if my best friend had committed the highest treason. The painter, on the other hand, received the news with a meanness of spirit verging on the offensive, tolerable only when he told me, in the reproving tones of a kindergarten teacher, 'I told you Fraester was shameless. He didn't even have the grit to stand up to those who can clearly do us more harm than good. And as a consequence, I'm afraid our poor Flemish peasant is now in even greater danger.'

I was beginning to tire of Cossini's protracted allusiveness. Influenced perhaps by the numerous crime novels

I've read and written in my lifetime, it seemed unfair that this impromptu detective never bothered to spell out his deductions for me. For example, I never understood how he knew Alikoshka Goliadkin had one arm, or what had led him to question Bogart's philanthropy so insistently and so soon. With respect to the danger which supposedly threatened Fraester, that afternoon Cossini showed a little more patience, resigned to struggling with an unbelievably gauche accomplice. As soon as I dared demand he be clearer, the painter sighed and steeled himself to explain what to him was more than obvious: by handing over his section of the manuscript, Fraester had enabled us to find out how much importance Bogart, and whoever was behind him, really attached to it. In fact, he added, there could only be two reasons why anyone might be interested in the palimpsest: either they actually wanted to know its contents, or else they already knew what it said and wished at all costs to prevent that information getting out. When I asked him what Fraester's decision had to do with all that, Cossini's reply was both horrendous and inescapable: 'If our friend Fraester suffers a fatal accident in the coming days, we'll know that what really interests these individuals in the baron's writing is ensuring it remains unknown. Moreover, I fear they won't shrink from eliminating anyone who's ever laid hands on it.'

Then, like someone hearing the threat in his own words echo back at him, he concluded, 'I know, my dear sir. It's clear you and I are pieces in the same game.'

A couple of weeks later Cossini rang me in London to tell me, with the glee of a competitor facing a new and complex challenge, that Fraester had died in the Arizona desert during the filming of the first and only movie he'd have appeared in under his own name. Needless to say, the news chilled me to the bone. I was almost angry the painter's prediction had been so accurate, as if he, too, were on the other side of the curtain now separating me from the rest of the world. What could we do now? At least Fraester had been able to enjoy the baron's money for a time, whereas we felt our very existence menaced by the possession of a manuscript which burned my hands like a letter bomb.

'Forgive my enthusiasm,' Cossini said as if reading my mind, 'but on some level I can't help admiring the baron's skill.'

By way of clarification, he added that he had thought long and hard about Fraester's part in Blok-Cissewsky's postscript, and concluded that, perhaps in expectation of his own execution, the baron had chosen the inept actor *knowing* he would hand over his part of the manual without a second thought. We should consider ourselves protagonists of an ingenious game of chess in which Fraester's murder should be interpreted as a calculated sacrifice by Blok-Cissewsky, a gambit through which the baron meant to show us our opponents' true colours and the importance they assigned the manuscript. On the other hand, added Cossini, if the baron had actually planned all this before dying we could rest easy, for it was certain the manual now in the hands of our dear Bogart would not give away anything compromising, and this led him to the conclusion that our texts were only what they appeared to be. All this, Cossini assured me, gave us precious time to make whatever move we wished, for Bogart and his friends would think carefully before resorting to their unorthodox methods to get their hands on our manuscripts and avoid our indiscretion.

A mixture of admiration and horror assailed me as the painter wove his version of events surrounding Fraester's death. All his reasoning seemed extremely sound, like one of those infallible declamations with which literary detectives unveil the murderer with watertight logic. However, as Cossini let himself be carried away with awe at the baron's phantom genius, I realized his ideas were entirely speculative, based on facts as impossible to verify as Blok-Cissewsky's foresight that Fraester would hand over his part of the manuscript or his conviction that Cossini and I would remain loyal to his memory, even to the detriment of our wallets. To this one had to add his even less believable (though exact) prophesies, such as Bogart's offer, the actor's prompt murder or simply the worrying fact that Cossini and I were still alive when our pursuers could have secured the manuscript by killing us to begin with. It's true, I thought, that the baron was a magnificent chess player, but in real life no one can anticipate a man's moves with the same precision that governs chess. For his part, Remigio Cossini must have also been a very ingenious player, but his passion for chess seemed to lead him to mistake the ambiguous laws of our existence with those ruling the giant board he had stamped on his brain.

'This all sounds very good, Mr Cossini,' I said, at last confident of his weakness. 'But did you ever wonder what would happen if Baron Blok-Cissewsky hadn't foreseen Fraester's betrayal and death? Why did the baron go to so much trouble when it would have been easier to deliver the information to the authorities himself? I think it would be better to leave it all in the hands of the police and forget the whole thing.'

Far from being offended by my suspicion, Remigio Cossini just laughed at my cowardly proposal. 'I understand your writerly doubts perfectly, my friend. I don't deny there's more imagination than certainty in my ideas, but they're all we have. For now, I can only assure you that Bogart isn't working for Israeli justice, that Adolf

Eichmann was a dead man the moment they arrested him and, at the same time, that nobody in his right mind would ever go to so much trouble gathering proof for a court which evidently doesn't need any. All this allows us to suppose Bogart is not a Nazi-hunter but just the opposite. Should that be so, I very much doubt the police can do anything about it. I thought at first the manuscript meant something personal to the baron, a sort of talisman someone else could use when he was gone.'

Knowing Cossini had at least a few certainties did little to calm me, for these, like his hypotheses, led our steps inexorably towards a pit where the monstrous open jaws of Humphrey Bogart lay in wait. Telling myself Fraester's death had been an accident did nothing to diminish my fear that something or someone round the next corner threatened us. After all, Cossini was right: in these circumstances it was better to err on the side of mistrust and hold to the darkest theories. Only that way could we retain a glimmer of hope that the ghost of Baron Woyzec Blok-Cissewsky, architect of our misfortunes, might also have bequeathed us some weapons for our defence.

'Now, my friend, we know what to expect,' the painter interrupted me towards the end of our conversation. 'These Polish notes are our life insurance. I suggest we put them in safe keeping and show no signs of trying to decipher them. I also recommend you take a holiday in the middle of nowhere. Later, if we're spared the same fate as Fraester, we'll meet again.'

And so saying he offered a perfunctory goodbye like someone ending the most trivial conversation.

It took me several days to digest completely Cossini's conclusions about Deman Fraester's death. Again I found it difficult to believe the baron had actually decided to sacrifice the actor in order to give us a kind of security, a breathing space in which to escape or to decide what to do with our lives. My own part of the manuscript was still in my hands, the hundred thousand Swiss francs I'd inherited were still in a dead man's bank account, and the memory of Bogart persisted in menacing every step I took. On the other hand, Adolf Eichmann's trial in Jerusalem was proceeding apace without need for further evidence, and it was difficult to imagine that anything or anyone was working to save him from the noose or to hasten his conviction. Many times, persuaded that Fraester's death had been accidental and Cossini's suspicions were unfounded, I thought of looking Bogart up to give him the baron's manuscript, but a trace of doubt, similar to what sometimes decides the outcome of a game of chess, led me to defer the handover indefinitely. Judging by the deathly silence since my last conversation with the painter, perhaps Cossini was right and the whole thing had fallen into a placid backwater; all the same it still seemed as precarious as a skiff in the middle of the ocean. In my opinion, there were still too many loose threads, and Cossini knew it. I often felt indignant that the pedantic, self-sufficient painter had not sought my help in untangling a game which clearly he had no intention of relinquishing. Whether he had done so to insult or protect me mattered little. I would show him Baron Blok-Cissewsky had been right in choosing me as well, by being the one to decipher the manuscript.

I should make it clear that, at least here, I had a certain advantage over Cossini. When I decided to take on his far-fetched idea that the baron had chosen each of us after carefully analysing our agility on the board of life, I began a tortuous analysis of my own aptitudes and limitations to find out what he might have seen in my mediocre existence which could have served his purposes. It no longer surprised me that the old man had chosen Fraester for his slowness of wit or the painter for his extraordinary perspicacity. As for me, I thought in the end, his reasons must centre on something as palpable as my old and slight connection to the field of cryptography. During the final months of the war, and perhaps in anticipation of my future role as literary impostor, I worked in the RAF communications office, where some of my colleagues were in charge of randomly rummaging through continental correspondence in search of cryptograms favourable or detrimental to the Allies. Romantic though it may sound, the job was actually astonishingly dull. I still don't know whether Cossini knew about that stage in my past and if he, like the baron, was secretly waiting for me to exert those virtues in our favour. All in all, what was really worrying was the feeling – almost the certainty – that Blok-Cissewsky had included me in his postscript for my probable ability to break codes like the one in his manual. I started to believe the hand of my former chess opponent pulled the strings of my life even from the next world, as if the deepest layers of my existence had always been at his mercy, spread out before his eyes like rickety pieces on an alabaster board.

Whatever the baron's real reasons for naming me one of his heirs, from then on I devoted my energies to deciphering the manuscript. And, I confess, it wasn't easy. To begin with, most of the text was written in Polish, so I had to rely on the good offices of someone better versed in that language than I to find out if there were any intentional irregularities. A friend at the publishing house informed me that the only noteworthy features of the manuscript were the author's atrocious spelling and startling knowledge of chess. It was to be expected that a German would make mistakes in a language not his own, but my slight knowledge of Blok-Cissewsky's virtues and manias, like my growing conviction that in this story nothing obvious would lead me anywhere, led me to reject the possibility of the baron's errors being mere spelling mistakes. And so, after exhausting all known resources for deciphering cryptograms, I went back to the publishing house and asked the translator for her help in finding a pattern in the spelling mistakes in the text. Just as I expected, the result was an old numerical constant which, if memory served, was one of the legacies of the First World War to members of the legendary British secret service.

Unfortunately, that information wasn't enough to decipher Blok-Cissewsky's manuscript. A code, my RAF colleagues used to explain, has the same functions as a labyrinth whose traps and hatches, numerous or not, each guard their own minotaur, protecting him from the rash hero with no Ariadne's thread. Like labyrinths, no code is impregnable, but there are those which require three-dimensional thinking, almost an initiatory knowledge, which in this case was limited by my not being able to get any further than I had in understanding the enigma. From then on, the application of the numerical code would come up only with gibberish which more than once made me think I'd never reach the door opening onto the heart of darkness.

I had no option but to resort to my old boss from the communications office. Colonel Ewan Campbell, who by this stage was squandering his old age in the Egyptology classrooms of the University of Edinburgh, came to my aid with boundless enthusiasm. No sooner had he glanced at the hieroglyphics my latest decipherment of the manuscript had elicited than he exclaimed, with the satisfaction of a philatelist coming across an eighteenth-century postal seal, 'Good God, Sergeant. This would have earned you promotion a few years ago.'

Campbell immediately began to explain that the baron's text was written in Wolpuk, a hermetic medieval code. 'You've no reason to know this,' Campbell added, 'but during the war Wolpuk was widely used by those responsible for the Amphitryon Project.'

For a second I feared the old academic had become as obscure as Cossini. Luckily, Colonel Campbell did not expect me to be fully aware of the ins and outs of espionage from a war which I had spent vetting heaps of folders and heart-rending love letters. The Amphitryon Project, the cryptographer went on, transporting us back to the RAF offices, had been one of the many failed attempts by Nazi officers opposed to Hitler's policies to destroy the regime from within. Ironically, said Campbell, the original idea for the project came from none other than Goering; not that he, as far as is known, had ever thought to betray Hitler, but because he initially came up with the idea of creating a little legion of lookalikes for the Führer and his generals, to serve as decoys in the event of a rout. Towards the end of the war, however, those responsible for the Amphitryon Project decided to use their impostors to replace some of the Reich's generals. But something went badly wrong in those prodigious machinations, and the general who had orchestrated the conspiracy and the majority of his impostors were accused of conspiring with Jews to assassinate the Führer, and they disappeared off the map in 1943.

I remember at that moment I was about to ask Colonel Campbell if he knew the name of the man in charge of Project Amphitryon, but realized in time that the question was unnecessary. Not that I feared disappointment. There was not a doubt in my mind that it would be none other than Thadeus Dreyer, and perhaps I didn't want to prolong a conversation which was unlikely to take me much further. Colonel Campbell had fallen silent, lost in memory or maybe waiting for me to invite him to pursue this path away from university routine. It was clear that this text in Wolpuk would obsess him as completely as whatever had led the baron to trace countless figures in the air in search of the one that would lead him to an exquisite checkmate. What harm could there be in giving a poor washed-up cryptographer the chance he craved to unravel a code which I'd never be able to crack on my own? He'd need only a small section of the manual, while I kept hold of the rest, and could boast to Cossini that I'd found the thread that would lead us out of the great labyrinth that had claimed the lives of Fraester and Baron Blok-Cissewsky.

'Amphitryon,' I confided smugly as soon as I recognized Remigio Cossini's voice at the other end of the line.

But his response seemed not to contain the slightest trace of alarm. Once again I had the impression my call fulfilled the painter's expectations with clockwork precision. He seemed to imply that I'd taken an exasperating length of time to get in touch with him. I'd wanted to surprise him and demonstrate that I, too, was capable of following my own trails successfully, that I could make my own moves in the game we'd begun against that sinister opponent of whom he spoke with absolute confidence based on intuition. But Cossini took my news calmly, perhaps with insulting condescension. As though my naming Amphitryon were the question of a curious student rather than a masterly declaration, the painter replied, 'Amphitryon. Delightful character, no doubt about it. There must be at least thirty plays based on that pathetic individual's story. I find Molière's extremely indecent. If you want my opinion, the one by Plautus is the best.'

Needless to say, shortly before phoning Cossini I'd taken the time to investigate who Amphitryon had been, and was prepared to explain in detail the story of that poor warrior who found himself supplanted in his conjugal bed by none other than Zeus. But now the irritatingly exact Cossini was giving me a lesson. Tired of his games and self-sufficiency, I blurted out my story of Wolpuk and the conspiracy headed years ago by General Dreyer. Too late. By the time I realized, the painter had interrupted me again with one of his disarming phrases: 'As for our friend Blok-Cissewsky, or whatever you want to call him, I'm afraid his Amphitryon doesn't rank among the happier versions.' And, he added, in his less than humble opinion, he'd have much preferred the name Hercules for Dreyer's project, since in his case it hadn't been gods trying to supplant mortals but the reverse.

So, I thought, profoundly dismayed, Maestro Remigio Cossini knew all about Blok-Cissewsky's past, and was off-hand enough about it to make dismissive asides. I was about to tell Cossini to go to hell when he confessed, with unaccustomed humility, that he hadn't been able to break the baron's code. He added, though, that he had always suspected the whole mess was linked to the time when the baron still used the name Thadeus Dreyer, even though he'd never believed the baron's death, almost twenty years after the war, had been a mere act of revenge by some neo-Nazi group. Anyone with a modicum of cunning should have been able to guess the manuscript contained some-thing more than historical information about Adolf Eichmann's crimes: most likely precise information, addresses and names, leading to whoever hid behind our fake Humphrey Bogart.

'I'm so glad you've deciphered the manuscript,' Cossini eventually murmured as if talking to himself. 'You've saved me a long, tiresome voyage. On the other hand, perhaps we're still in time to save an innocent man from the gallows.'

After that, Cossini sank into an expectant silence which left me feeling utterly disappointed at being back in my slighted, Sancho Panchesque pose. Cossini's last words were the most depressing, since he obviously took it for granted that I already knew what the baron's manuscript contained, and was counting on my skill at deciphering for our survival as well as that of some unspecified individual whose fate also appeared to depend on me. Now, for the first time since we'd met, the maestro expected me to shed the final light on our dilemma.

'To be perfectly frank, Mr Cossini,' I had to confess, 'I haven't finished translating the manuscript yet. At the moment all I've figured out is that the baron used an old military code called Wolpuk.'

I expected the painter, on hearing this confession, to heave a sigh of resignation before launching into a new set of instructions with the patience of one reminded afresh of his apprentice's stupidity. But this time my words provoked a rare burst of rage: 'If you haven't broken the code,' he exclaimed, 'how the hell do you know about Project Amphitryon?'

Remigio Cossini had caught me out. I can't think why I didn't dare demand there and then his own sources of information: how it was possible he also knew about the Amphitryon Project if he hadn't been able to crack the Wolpuk code. In any case, he obviously realized I'd resorted to a third party for help in deciphering the manuscript, and that was a flagrant infringement of the tacit code of caution we'd imposed since the start.

'I thought it was Fraester who was supposed to play the idiot in this story,' Cossini said, abandoning his habitual coolness. 'I sincerely hope you don't come to regret your blunder. The problem with playing chess using human pieces is that they tend not to respect the most basic rules.'

And that concluded our strange connection forever.

Days later, in complete vindication of Remigio Cossini's fears, I discovered the fake Bogart had arrived in Great Britain to conclude the matter we'd thought resolved by Fraester's blood. And this time, needless to say, his methods were much less subtle than during our Geneva encounter.

The briefest of phone calls from Colonel Campbell was enough to alert me to the fact that something had finally broken the deceptive calm the painter and I had been trying to sustain. In a tone reminiscent of the stammering secretary who'd admitted us into the executor's office all those months ago, my old communications boss told me he'd at last solved the baron's cryptogram, and was therefore delighted to invite me to visit him in Edinburgh, where we could decode the rest of the manuscript together. No need for Cossini's dazzling intuition to understand not only that Wolpuk's evasions remained entirely impenetrable to the old colonel, but that beside him at that very moment hovered the perpetual American cigarette so familiar to Blok-Cissewsky's heirs, straight and threatening as the barrel of a gun. My reply, then, was briefer than the old colonel's invitation: poorly feigning enthusiasm at the news of his cracking the code, I said I'd catch the first train to Edinburgh that very afternoon, so we could spend as much time as needed to decode the manuscript, which, I lied, was unlikely to yield more than a few matters of historical interest for a novel I was thinking of writing.

I always wondered how Bogart managed to get down to London that very instant. The logical thing would be to think that Colonel Campbell, contrary to what I first suspected, had been alone when he called from his Edinburgh house or in the company of another no less ominous thug. I think, however, the only face I'll ever be able to give the members of that enigmatic army is Humphrey Bogart's. Even today, when misfortune puts the actor's movies or posters in my path, I shudder and feel as if each image was a separate man, one of those endless clones which my brain conjures to represent the seat of my fear and give it an individual face.

Be that as it may, the fact was that Bogart was no longer in Edinburgh but in London and, displaying an ability even Cossini seemed to have underestimated, he had easily divined that Colonel Campbell's phone call would take me not to the Scottish capital but to Heathrow airport; he welcomed me at the terminal doors with the smile of a hunter watching a frightened animal break from the undergrowth. Before I could even pay the taxi driver, he had bundled me into the back seat of another car, whose driver hardly batted an eyelid at our skirmish. Then, at a wink in the rear-view mirror from Bogart, the car pulled away.

'You seem to be in quite a hurry to leave us, my friend,' growled Bogart, looking for something in the pockets of his jacket. 'Poor Colonel Campbell will be so upset by your lack of interest.' And he put one of his inevitable cigarettes in his mouth.

The whole situation began to seem tedious rather than terrifying, and might have become actually boring had not Bogart finally lit the cigarette I'd come to think of as an incombustible prop. That apparently trivial gesture was enough to send a shudder through me, not from the vague fear I'd felt over the last few months, but from the alto-gether more powerful conviction that Bogart was part of a secret army trained to protect a dark king, beyond the reach of law, immune from justice or death like the absolute ruler of evil. Perhaps he was only one of many copies of Humphrey Bogart, who could only mark himself out by refusing to light his cigarette, a small distinction between himself and others more resigned to personifying the terror of ubiquity. In some secret archive there must have been a series of absurdly similar records, an infinity of possible Bogarts, where some poor soul has unsuccessfully tried to make a single person out of their slightly different features, mannerisms, vices, ways of walking, making love or killing. And maybe a few shelves higher was a dossier bearing my name, or Remigio Cossini's, waiting for someone to send it to the oblivion of the shredder.

Gradually the taxi left the area around the airport and entered the teeming city which, for some reason, felt as if it was about to be blacked out. All those lights, car horns and voices seemed to be aware that at any moment a cloak of darkness and silence would extinguish them. In fact, it didn't take long for the city to blur into a succession of ever more vague trees and shadows. Without my noticing, we had crossed the centre and were now nearing the suburbs, where the final solution Cossini had long expected surely awaited me. At one point I thought of asking Bogart how he had guessed Cossini and I hadn't given up trying to unravel the enigma, but the distant hope that the painter might still be safe kept me quiet.

However, as if he too could read my thoughts, Bogart said, in his world-weary way, 'Your friend the painter is fine, my dear sir. He's merely suffered one of his recurrent nervous breakdowns. We gave him a little help going back to the place he never should have left.'

As he spoke he took from his jacket pocket a photograph I found extremely disconcerting: Remigio Cossini, or someone who could certainly have been his double, sitting at a table in what looked like a hospital refectory.

'Didn't you know?' Bogart affected an ill-concealed sarcasm. 'That's a shame. I should have warned you from the start what kind of man you were getting involved with.'

I didn't answer, silenced by the exhaustion of fear and the photograph. Perhaps I should have doubted my executioner's words once more, dismissing the photo and the supposed madness of the only truly lucid man I'd ever known. But by that point I was frankly sick of doubting, and was prepared wholeheartedly to believe that human wreck actually was Cossini. But I resisted the conclusion that the entire Blok-Cissewsky story was merely a psychopath's invention. The only thing that sank in was the fact that Bogart and his men had plunged Cossini into despair, an old or brand-new insanity from which nothing

168

could save him. The photograph shook in my hands like a telegram bringing news of a comrade's death on the battle-field, read and reread with the desolation of someone searching for the full vein of tragedy in the chill of an official document. The painter wore a dressing-gown which must once have been white, but was now so dirty and threadbare that it alone was enough to undermine any faith in the institution; a slight shadow around the bottom of his face suggested an incipient beard, so much at odds with his former appearance. In front of him, on the table, a chess set with unusually large pieces awaited the next move.

'It's his turn,' Bogart explained, taking the picture back and returning it to his sinister warren of pockets, 'but he's been like that for a couple of days. The doctors say it could take him an eternity to make his next move.'

A burst of silent laughter erupted from the icy depths of his posturing, its only outward sign being the reddening glow of his cigarette. Fatigue began to claim me again. Rage bubbled in the pit of my stomach, as if trapped there. Cossini's defeat and the prospect of remembering him that way for ever – incapable and undone by the rules of a game too human to be resolved by the resources of his mind – left me completely at the mercy of our opponents, and resigned to never knowing whether Baron Blok-Cissewsky had planned our ruin or whether, instead, we had disappointed him.

As though enjoying the pained silence of my thoughts, Bogart also stayed quiet while the taxi drove through an increasingly dream-like landscape. At some point I let my gaze wander to the rear-view mirror and noticed the driver's eyes fixed on me, not with Bogart's sadistic delight but rather as if he recognized in me a slight assurance, a remote possibility which his partner, distracted by the act of smoking and lighting one cigarette after the other, hadn't been able to distinguish. Suddenly, stopped at a red light, the driver broke the silence and spoke to Bogart in German, ordering him to do something with the iron decision of an old military man addressing a subordinate.

While Bogart agreed to the driver's instructions I watched the foggy streets of London pass by like a child tired of listening to his parents' daily rows. Vast parks like military cemeteries, roundabouts and pedestals invaded by unsavoury characters hawking their newspapers; ever broader, more suburban avenues bringing us closer to marginal territory. The fog appeared to thicken until I realized with a start that my breath on the window was turning the cityscape into the set of a bad expressionist movie. I felt the fear evident in my breath no longer belonged to me, as if I too were about to transmigrate into another body, abandoning this one as no longer my concern. The monotonous repetition of buildings persisted – I tried to convince myself that the taxi was driving round in circles to confuse me. But that idea was also quickly consigned to the list of silly fantasies my literary imagination devised to give me false hopes. By this stage I'd given myself up for dead, reduced to a ghost, an extra hired by a famous producer to pad out the briefest of crowd scenes.

The taxi eventually drove into an area of vacant lots and ramshackle buildings. Though night had closed in on us, for a moment I was transported back to that Swiss afternoon when, in another city, on another journey, Remigio Cossini told me fate had pitched us into a story whose murky depths were only now being revealed. Maybe Bogart himself, or one of his innumerable clones, had followed us that day from the station in a car similar to the one now driving me to the outskirts of London. Perhaps he'd taken orders from the same fake driver, both of them sure the two travellers whose faces they barely knew from descriptions or photographs would sooner or later be completely at their mercy. Our futile resistance would seem nothing more than the short-lived buzz of a bluebottle chased around a windowless house.

The car and my companions' conversation both stopped at the side of the motorway. Night had swallowed dusk like a voracious Russian winter, and Cossini's image was also enveloped in my memory by a mantle of shadows. Bogart hesitated a moment before speaking to me. Something in his conversation with the driver had disturbed very slightly the façade of jaded certainty, which I suppose he'd spent months sustaining on my behalf. For a few seconds he stared at me as if someone had suddenly told him I wasn't the same man who'd entered the narrow confines of his power minutes before. I glimpsed in his eyes the mixture of surprise and annoyance shown by opera-goers when told their favourite diva is indisposed and in the performance about to begin her part will be sung by an unknown but promising soprano. That doubt, however, soon disappeared.

'I want to believe,' he said, extinguishing his cigarette in the car's ashtray, 'that your share of the manuscript is in your suitcase. In any case, you know we'll find it sooner or later.'

I felt, as he stubbed out his cigarette, that Bogart was also banishing the doubts that had previously begun to oppress him in his conversation with the driver. He again spoke with the authority he had used to humiliate Baron Blok-Cissewsky's three heirs months before. He was incapable of doubt. On the other hand, the way he reluctantly took a revolver from his pocket fitted his role perfectly. He didn't have to tell me to step out of the car. In my overwrought imagination I'd run through this scene countless times from the moment my executioner appeared at the airport. Or maybe before, when Bogart first stepped into my life as if according to the logic of a bad novel, the kind that always ends the same way, on a cold, dark night, with the silent complicity of an embankment where no one would hear the shot, let alone the dry thud of a body hitting the ground, blood seeping from the back of the neck. Not knowing how or when, I had at some point entered the scene of my own murder with an irritating familiarity, almost grateful things could no longer happen any other way. Maybe that's why I hardly noticed the blast of wind hitting my face that night as I opened the car door. For a moment I thought the driver again muttered something which sounded like an order, but it was too late to hear him: I was kneeling on the ground, and my eyes had already closed at the unmistakable sound of an expert hand cocking the firing pin of a revolver.

I don't deny the years have sharpened some edges of my consciousness, but it has also been exposed to time's devastating power to harden our opinions and render us impervious to any stimulus from outside. In the years since I last spoke to Remigio Cossini, I have tried to recover a degree of sensitivity to the arts which has, nevertheless, persistently eluded me with the slippery wiles of a deep-sea fish. Journalists are forever asking my opinion of one of the many paintings or symphonies I mention in my novels. I always improvise an answer and try to appear as if I actually care about what I'm saying. I don't mention the interminable afternoons spent listening to arias I find deathly boring or wandering through galleries that excite me as much as planting a kiss on a lobster's shell. Of course, I never mention the canvas that Remigio Cossini, perhaps foreseeing the danger threatening him after my wrong move with Colonel Campbell, arranged to have sent to me upon his death, which occurred in 1964, three years after the events I've been trying to relate. The painting is obviously a forgery, modelled in its turn on a kind of fraud. It's a faithful copy of the famous *Man Seated in a Dark Room* attributed to an imitator of Rembrandt, and I feel no need to explain why Cossini was so attached to the painting that he kept it to the end of his life.

The painter's bequest, like Baron Blok-Cissewsky's manuscript, contained an assumption verging on the macabre: his uncanny conviction that, in spite of everything, I'd survive the fatal destiny he'd been unable to avoid. Whether he imagined the way in which my life was to outlast his own, and whether later, in his madness, he managed to discover Eichmann had been sentenced and hanged in Tel Aviv two years after being arrested in Argentina, are details I'll never ascertain. Even so, whatever his reasons for predicting my salvation, when I received the painting I realized my unfortunate friend hadn't thought twice before deciding I should be the one to receive it. When I first looked at that meditative figure in oils, imprisoned in the most dramatic chiaroscuro, I thought this singular legacy was also a kind of posthumous cryptogram, one of the many elusive, seemingly false courses the painter had followed. Then I thought of him, in that place to which Bogart's torture had consigned him, perhaps numb with cold at the end of countless numbered corridors, eternally silent before his chessboard, wrapped in that dirty dressing-gown. I remembered this three years later when I received his work, and I felt unworthy of a soft bed and luxurious flat in Notting Hill, which in other circumstances I would have thought comfortable but which then seemed insuperable obstacles to understanding the painting, where the missing piece to my story might lie.

For once, uncharacteristically, I was only half mistaken. Everything in the picture was a veiled allusion to the huge dilemma Baron Blok-Cissewsky had left us years before. As one would expect from a mind like his, Cossini had taken great care when playing his last card, perhaps hoping that, at least once, I'd manage to rise to the level of his machinations. No coded text, no phrase hidden under the canvas, would have been worthy enough of him for me to bother seeking it out. The canvas had to be in fact an evocation of Cossini himself inviting me to rethink, step by step, everything he had said to me long ago. It was as if he realized that he had at some point given me a loose thread to cling to after he was gone.

It took me several days to atune my mind to the wavelength Cossini required from the kingdom of the dead. It was almost a pleasure to withdraw as far as possible from my publishing commitments and reclaim for a few moments the grey solitude I'd once found unbearable. Gradually I managed to block out my flat's intrusive luxury and confront Cossini's painting with the energy of someone refusing to wake from a dream in which an enigma that has tormented him since childhood is about to be solved. One morning, I discovered my brain working at a speed I'd never experienced before, and I found I'd discovered in my memories the sentence Cossini had wanted me to remember. In our last telephone conversation, the painter had spoken of a tiresome journey I might have spared him by deciphering the baron's manuscript. Perhaps that afternoon, fearing Cossini's disappointment, I had shut that phrase away in the confused area of the mind where all allusions to a journey seem prescient metaphors for death.

But Cossini, I knew, did not have a poetic soul. His journey, therefore, had to be real. Where to? Where would he have found the part of the baron's truth he once believed encoded in our manuscript? Surely, as a consequence of our last conversation and Colonel Campbell's betrayal, the painter, too, had been captured at a railway station or airport, even if Cossini had not at first been fleeing a fate which, as Bogart had been careful to point out to me, would have caught up with him sooner or later. No. He must have been aiming to find out the truth, before others plunged him into the eternal uncertainty of his madness.

Geneva, London, Vienna. I visited all those possible chess squares in our private cartography thousands of times from my Notting Hill solitude. More than once, over the last three years, destiny had brought me back to those places. Each city, each face and each word spoken in an unknown language held for me that dockside chill which makes us feel exiled from even ourselves. Now, though, my mental evocation of those places gave me no sign of enclosing the minotaur Cossini must have been searching for, until one day, when I was about to abandon my efforts, a chance event brought me to the one place that had completely escaped my notice. The light came not coded in the battered ciphers of memory, but in one of those loathsome telegrams my publishers sent advising me of another insufferable tour to promote my books. Out of habit, almost out of contempt, I always need to get drunk before finding out the latest destination to which my increasingly unpleasant literary duties would consign me. But now some intuition told me this envelope, identical to so many others, had to be different. I tore it open and saw the longed-for name of Frankfurt rising before me, blindingly powerful like a solar explosion. That city's name seared my brain, immediately returning me to my memory of the baron's will. Perhaps misled by his customary disdain for the obvious, the painter must have initially assumed that the baron's moves were limited to the three names in his enigmatic postscript. Only later had he glimpsed the possibility that our trio of heirs was in fact probably a quartet, the last member of which must be located in Frankfurt, in the sanatorium in aid of which the baron had directed his belongings to be auctioned. Could this be the journey the painter had tried to make after our last talk? Or infected by his ghost, could I have reached the conclusion independently? No one and nothing could answer these questions. But that didn't keep me from seizing on that unique and fragile Ariadne's thread to carry on down my own path towards the truth.

Five days later I landed at Frankfurt airport, prepared to visit every sanatorium in the city until I found traces of Blok-Cissewsky's will. The enterprise seemed so absurd that most people would never have begun it, but I was convinced my intuitions would gradually fall into place as I approached the destination to which, in some way, I'd been heading ever since my grotesque odyssey began.

It would be pointless going into the details of my long detour through the sanatoria of Frankfurt asking if they had had anything to do with Baron Blok-Cissewsky or

General Thadeus Dreyer, handing out money and consulting extensive lists of inmates, not knowing exactly what name I was looking for. Suffice it to say that those weeks went by as if outside time, as if my obsession with following the painter's thwarted steps had led me to an end of the earth where the only compass was my own anxiety. When I at last found the place I'd been looking for, I felt I'd become the last grain of sand in the giant hourglass that my life and Cossini's had occupied since the death of Baron Blok-Cissewsky.

Not really a home, it was one of those dirty, dilapidated houses where vagrants rather than elderly people end their days, anonymous buildings whose administrators soak the social-security budget for more money than they actually spend on the inmates. Practically impervious to this or any other kind of twist in the baron's story, I was scarcely surprised to learn the baron had not only donated the value of his Geneva belongings to the place but had for many years been considered its most generous benefactor. The man in charge of the home was almost as old as the majority of its residents, but although he started off by saying he had trouble remembering, a few marks were enough to refresh his memory. After I'd followed the baron's steps so far and squandered my life in the effort I became ruthless in my pursuit of the truth of the matter. Thanks to my possession by Cossini's ghost, the mechanisms that would link the actions and death of my old chess opponent were already assembled in my head. It needed only a little push from the administrator to get them into gear. I was hardly worried that this final truth now depended on an old, disreputable doctor who surely knew less than he'd like me to think. Undoubtedly he'd let his memories surface slowly, hoping anxiety would encourage my largesse. But I was no longer in a hurry to hear him, so I waited patiently until he decided to tell me his version of events.

'This will be the last time I speak to strangers of the late Mr Blok-Cissewsky's affairs,' the old man warned me that afternoon. 'He always asked us to be discreet about his business. Furthermore, I don't think it's proper to tell so many people about it.'

He spoke bitterly, with something like the hurt pride of a jilted lover added to the melodramatic tone of someone too fond of pulp fiction. His story was perhaps as ambiguous as everything else related to Baron Blok-Cissewsky, but towards the end I could detect a sincerity hitherto conspicuous by its absence during my investigation. Those words contained nothing I now consider a startling revelation. Nevertheless, I think this time the administrator's story made me feel that at last light was being shed in some if not all of the corners kept in darkness over the last few years.

Baron Blok-Cissewsky, the old man began to tell me, had written to him shortly after the war, asking after one of the inmates, a certain Viktor Kretzschmar, who had arrived in the sanatorium in 1937 after a four-year confinement in Viennese prisons for causing a railway accident in which dozens of people died. Blok-Cissewsky begged complete discretion from his correspondent, and generously promised to cover that particular inmate's expenses, so long as he was kept punctually informed of his condition. At that time, the administrator went on to explain, old Kretzschmar was a wreck, a human ruin who alternated between ever less frequent moments of lucidity and pro- longed outbursts of rage. Of course, the home gladly accepted the baron's offer, and from then on exchanged regular reports on the resident Kretzschmar for significant sums of money which were supposedly spent on the old man's upkeep and treatment. Much later, in May 1960, the baron showed up at the sanatorium, bringing no lug- gage except an old chessboard, and insisted on speaking to the inmate. The words, entreaties and barely suppressed anger the baron employed to try to bring Kretzschmar to his senses were all in vain. He was so desperate for the old man to play him at chess that the administrator would have been hard put to say which of the two old men deserved to be confined in the sanatorium. Blok-Cissewsky stayed several weeks and persisted in his futile quest until the day the press reported Adolf Eichmann's arrest in the city of Buenos Aires. Accustomed to the baron's phlegmatic personality, the administrator was still unable to explain the explosion of rage and anguish that piece of news provoked in his benefactor.

'He seemed possessed,' he assured me. 'When he saw the Nazi criminal's face on television, he started to scream that the man wasn't Eichmann, and swore he'd make sure the whole world learned the truth.'

The administrator didn't know for certain what 'truth' the baron was referring to so vehemently, but added that he'd heard him assure Kretzschmar he knew where the real Eichmann was to be found, and was going to prevent an injustice from being committed.

'Only he can play like that,' the baron told the scarecrow, brandishing in his face a handful of newspaper cuttings and tatty chess bulletins.

Kretzschmar, obviously, didn't even blanch at the promises made by the baron, who had no choice but to leave the sanatorium after he'd told the administrator as if talking to himself, 'I gave that man his life, sir, but I stole his soul. To tell the truth, today I'd give anything to return it to him.'

Whether the baron was referring to Adolf Eichmann or someone else is something neither the administrator nor I could ever deduce. The next day Blok-Cissewsky left the city, and only a few days later, coinciding with the news of his death, the administrator received a visit from a stranger who thrust a large sum of money at him in exchange for a promise that he would never tell anyone else about what had gone on between Kretzschmar and the baron. If he refused, the visitor added, they would ensure that he, too, disappeared, even more completely than Blok-Cissewsky.

When I heard that part of the story, I extracted an old photo of Humphrey Bogart from my pocket and asked my interlocutor if this was the man who had threatened him. 'That's him,' he murmured unperturbed, and then, more quietly, 'He killed him, didn't he?'

I didn't want to substantiate his suspicions then. By that stage it was as futile to search out the baron's flesh-and-blood murderer as it was to expect anything more of the administrator. Old Kretzschmar, it seemed, had died shortly after Adolf Eichmann's execution, and it seems that by then no one was left alive who could probe the story more deeply. I resigned myself to thinking that, in certain cases, clues and labyrinths led only to small spaces lit exclusively by minimal, personal truths. Perhaps we are condemned to keep searching for absolute truth, ever frustrated by those titbits of explanation with which the sour architect who rules over this endless labyrinth deigns to placate us from time to time.

As if stirred by the gloomy tenor of my thoughts, the administrator suddenly broke the soporific silence to which his tale had given way. His face betrayed an uneasy sadness and, to close the proceedings, he stood up, took a faded book from a bureau and offered it with the words: 'I'll sell it to you, sir. The baron left it before he departed. It's the last memento we have of him.'

And with that he walked me to the door and asked me bluntly not to look him up again.

Nothing could be more unpleasant than inquiring into a murderer's reasons for deciding at a given moment to spare one's life. Try as we may to adduce heroic or divine justification, logic inevitably leads us to the most humiliating possibility of all: contempt. On that night in London, did Bogart and the man driving the car really think my life wasn't even worth a bullet and a pinch of gunpowder? Sometimes I wonder if it wasn't also a minimal rebellion by those two men to divert death and thus rebel against God, the ubiquitous, omnipotent player who insists on reducing everyone, them included, to the state of miserable chess pieces. Whatever the truth of it, they decided to send me to a circle of hell where the torments are too insufferable and familiar for them to allow the easy exit of death.

Whom should I thank or blame for my survival? Whatever the answer, I'm the one who comes out the loser. The eternal second I spent with Bogart's revolver at my back was not only an encounter with the precariousness of life, but a moment of clarity which assumed its true dimensions only years later, when I spoke to the sanatorium administrator in Frankfurt. That night, as I was driven through London suburbs, even when I didn't know Blok-Cissewsky's precise motives for courting death to save a man like Adolf Eichmann, I began to sense his innermost reasons, those which all men have shared since the beginning of time. I now know that sometimes mere mortals accumulate enough rage to rebel against the gods, but on occasion the gods allow us to return home after they've usurped our beds and loved our wives.

There he was, then, a pawn of the shadowy player so admired by Remigio Cossini, ready to annihilate me with the same insouciance with which his boss, the driver of the car – perhaps the real Adolf Eichmann – must years ago have ordered the execution of millions of human beings. But that night, at the other's insistence, Bogart allowed the pieces to move in another direction. I don't know for certain what ideas went through his head. I only know that suddenly, instead of the shot, I heard one of his characteristic sighs of boredom and saw him return his revolver to the pocket of his trenchcoat. Then, while Bogart closed the car door behind him, the driver sarcastically suggested, without disguising his strong German accent, 'Do us a favour, my friend, write about this. It'll make an amusing story.' And with that he drove off, letting the engine drown a burst of laughter which still weighs on my soul.

Even if I haven't exactly accepted that invitation, to some extent I have become what they hoped. Although I now sign my books with my own name, in a way I still write what others want me to write, and I tell myself one day I'll have the guts to rebel and search out the gunshot Bogart aborted in London. Gradually I've begun to walk the streets, hiding behind ridiculous dark sunglasses. They may save me from being pursued by the press, but not from the sound of footsteps following me wherever I go, never allowing me a moment's rest, or the feeling of distance we need when we sense the world so close it seems to be suffocating us. I go into a bar and drink until I'm drunk or until, in my delirium, a figure appears and looks menacingly at the waiter so he'll refuse to keep serving me. Not angry, not contemptuous: I look at my imaginary guardian and in the gloom of the bar see Bogart's eyes, friendly and aloof, as if it was not him but one of his infinite reflections who'd spared my life. Frequently, when constant travelling leaves me exhausted for a couple of days in my apartment, I think of Baron Blok-Cissewsky, curse him and try to write down his maddening story on pages which promptly feed my fire. Among my mementoes of those ill-fated times, I still have the book the asylum administrator gave me after revealing the precise circumstances of Baron Blok-Cissewsky's ruin. It's just an old military yearbook containing a photograph of a group of officers of the Reich during the inauguration of Treblinka prison camp. In the centre, according to the caption, is a smiling General Thadeus Dreyer, flanked on his left by Staff Sergeant Alikoshka Goliadkin, and on his right by a certain Franz T. Kretzschmar, lieutenant of the Ninth Engineers Corps. Could that man be the son of the old man in Frankfurt whom Blok-Cissewsky had protected since the war? What did that engineer have to do with the Amphitryon Project or with Colonel Adolf Eichmann? Unfortunately, my intuition in no way matches the ill-fated Remigio Cossini's. Therefore, as the man who once spared my life wanted, my only choice is to seek an answer in the treacherous realm of my own imagination, the place where every story and every word lead inevitably to deceit.

Ignacio Padilla

San Pedro Cholula, 1999

Daniel Sanderson has argued more than once in his defence that his books don't emerge from history. They come from the generous spaces left in its wake as it spreads over the lives of men and nations. However, I believe such an argument invites others to seek out history in the empty spaces he often leaves us in his fiction.

The Adolf Eichmann bibliography is very extensive, but most of the information can be found in *The Capture and Trial of Adolf Eichmann* by Moshe Pearlman and Hannah Arendt's now legendary *Eichmann in Jerusalem: A Report on the Banality of Evil*. The facts which interest us are few: after the fall of the Reich Adolf Eichmann eventually escaped from Germany under the name of Otto Heninger and after extensive travels through Asia Minor settled down in Argentina, passing himself off as one Richard Klement. He was arrested in Buenos Aires in May 1960, tried in Jerusalem between April and December 1961, and finally hanged in Tel Aviv on 31 May 1962. All in all, despite the numerous confessions and eye-witness accounts presented during the trial, considerable doubt has remained as to the identity of the man who climbed an Israeli scaffold after one of the most dramatic trials in history.

As for General Thadeus Dreyer and the Amphitryon Project, the truth is more difficult to establish. There is some material on a proposed replacement project orchestrated by Hermann Goering in the first months of the war as a possible way to undermine the power of Heinrich Himmler, his eternal rival within the Reich. Little is known, however, about those directly responsible for the project, which was in effect broken up in 1943 as a conspiracy against the regime, involving collaboration with Jews. Among the men closest to Goering there was an officer of Austrian extraction called Thadeus Dreyer, who was decorated with the Iron Cross for bravery in the Piave and who disappeared in May 1943. The figure of Dreyer appears in what could be the photograph to which Sanderson refers in the last part of his book, although it was taken not in Treblinka, but probably in the back yard of the Gestapo's headquarters, and was published not in a military yearbook but as a centre spread in a special issue of *Der Stürmer*. The young man next to the officer is in fact called Franz T. Kretzschmar, someone listed among the war dead as killed during Operation Barbarossa. Whatever his fate, one cannot deny the young lieutenant's astonishing physical similarity to images of Thadeus Dreyer preserved from the time he returned to Austria as a First World War hero, and that is why it's not so far-fetched to suggest they might be father and son. Did young Kretzschmar participate in Hermann Goering's policy of substitutes under the aegis of General Dreyer? Could he be the one, as Sanderson suggests, who paid for the crimes of Adolf Eichmann with his life, prisoner of a past and of a face not his own? A remarkable chess player, Eichmann never denied his identity during his trial in Jerusalem, but that doesn't disprove Sanderson's conjectures. On the other hand, I doubt Kretzschmar would have kept silent about his identity in order to offer his father or superior officer protection he didn't need. It is more likely that Kretzschmar's silence in Jerusalem stemmed from the impostor's or bastard son's desire to wreak vengeance on the man who probably transformed him into merely another pawn on the huge chessboard of war. Dreyer himself said as much at the time with an anguish that only made sense in a father, lover or god betrayed by the error of his ways: he had given life to that man, but stolen his soul. That soul whose single and secret name we can reclaim only in death.

Salamanca, 1998–San Pedro Cholula, 1999

A NOTE ABOUT THE AUTHOR

Ignacio Padilla was born in Mexico City in 1968. He is the author of several award-winning novels and short story collections, including *La catedral de los ahogados* and *Subterráneos*, and he won Spain's prestigious Premio Primavera award for *Shadow Without a Name*. Ignacio Padilla stands at the forefront of the literary movement 'Crack', rediscovering the ambition of the Latin-American masters. He is the cultural attaché at the Mexican Embassy in London.